BLACK
Angels

LLOYD WILLIAMS

ISBN: 978-1-4834-6277-6 (sc)
ISBN: 978-1-4834-6276-9 (e)

Lulu Publishing Services rev. date: 1/6/2017

CHAPTER 1

August 14, 2014

Rogue police officers Gary Cooper and Steven Headley received information over the dispatch; there was excessive noise from a party in a residential neighborhood on Provost Avenue in Bellport, NY. It could possibly involve drug usage and underage alcohol consumption.

Their interest wasn't really the noise, the drugs, or the booze, though. Dispatch informed them that some of the party-goers were children of members of the Black Lives Matter organization led by activist Robert Carter. Cooper and Headley wanted to set an example and intimidate Carter and his protégés.

Officer Cooper put the police cruiser in park, and both officers exited the car. While walking up the driveway of the house in question, Officer Cooper towered over his nondescript partner, Officer Headley, who was 5'9, with brown hair and brown eyes. Officer Headley was the epitome of antisocial. He was so detached from reality and such a stubborn spirit to work with that Cooper was the only officer willing to work with him; he was, literally, Headley's only friend. He was antisocial, but his partner, Officer Cooper, got to see a different side of him—a sinister side.

While walking up the driveway, both officers could hear people partying inside the residence: raucous laughter, people chattering, and above it all, the smash hit "Empire State Of Mind" by Jay-Z and Alicia

Keys. Officer Cooper would bet anything that the volume was on maximum and the speakers were throbbing. As they stood outside the front door, they could see dancing silhouettes through the living room curtains.

Officer Headley banged on the door.

"I have a joke for you," he said, while they waited for someone to answer.

"Is it better than the last one?" Officer Cooper asked.

Headley's eyes narrowed.

"You didn't like my last joke?"

Cooper grinned when Headley acted offended.

"Not really."

"Then let me redeem myself: Why do blacks play basketball so well?"

"I don't know. Why don't you tell me?" Cooper asked, indifference in his tone.

"Because they steal, shoot, and run."

Both men burst into laughter.

Cooper wiped a tear from his eye. "I'm not going to lie; that was a good one." He grinned. Once their laughter started to die out, the officers noticed that no one had come to the door. "Why hasn't anyone come to the door yet?"

"Did you even knock?" Officer Cooper asked.

"You were standing right here."

"People never seem to acknowledge when you knock. Let me show you how to knock on a door and get a response." Officer Cooper proceeded to lift his hand and bang on the door several times.

Within seconds, a slim, young black male, wearing a white T-shirt, appeared at the door. He smiled at first, but then his smile vanished once he saw a perturbed Officer Cooper.

"Oh man. I thought it was Ronald with the booze. How can I help you, officer?" Judging from the smell of his breath, slurred speech, and vacant gaze in his brown eyes, it was obvious that he had already had enough to drink.

"I got a call about a disturbance," Officer Cooper said.

"A disturbance. We aren't being loud; it must have been my next door neighbors that called you," he said.

The young man's parents were out of town for a few days, so he'd figured it was the opportune time to throw a party. His neighbors were an elderly married couple who could not sleep through the voices and the music from the party, though. They had called the police on them three times already this evening, every call just minutes apart.

"Step aside, young man," Officer Cooper said, as he took a step forward.

Although the young man was inebriated, he still knew his rights. He was not going to let Officer Cooper intimidate him. "Do you have a warrant? If not, you are not allowed in," he said.

The officer decided to use diplomacy, for now. But he would return. "Listen, just keep the noise down and lower the music a little, and don't give me a reason to come back. Got it?" Officer Cooper said.

The young man nodded in agreement.

As the officers turned and walked away, they noticed a baby-faced African-American male walking in their direction, with a case of beer in his hand. Officer Cooper intentionally bumped into him, causing the case of beer to fall and the bottles to break.

"Hey! Watch where you're going, man!"

"Excuse me?" Cooper said.

"You heard what the hell I said!" He pointed at Officer Cooper. "Now look what you've done!"

"Maybe you need to learn how to speak to an officer," Cooper said. His face began to turn red.

"Maybe you need to get a pair of glasses, you blind fuck!"

Headley intervened. "Who the fuck do you think you're talking to?"

Officer Cooper reached for his night stick. "What was that, motherfucker?"

As his eyes fell on the nightstick, the kid decided to choose his words a little more carefully. He should have known better; he'd heard about an impulsive cop in his neighborhood lately. As implausible as it might sound, the cop seemed to be using young black men as target practice recently.

"He's a pussy," Headley shouted.

"Not so tough anymore, huh? I should beat your motherfucking ass. That would teach you some respect."

"Listen, officer," called the kid at the door with the white T-shirt, "it's no big deal. He's sorry."

"Shut your damn mouth!" Cooper shouted.

The young man at the door was not stupid, like his friend Ronald; he was twenty-two and wanted to live to see his twenty-third birthday, so he didn't utter another word.

"Let me see some identification," Cooper said to the hot-headed kid.

He pulled out his wallet, then furnished Officer Cooper with his identification.

Officer Cooper scrutinized his date of birth.

"Officer Headley, what is today's date?"

"August fourteenth, Officer Cooper."

"Who are you speaking to?" Ronald asked

Officer Cooper did the math on his hand, then grinned at the kid whose identification he held. "Ronald, today's date is August fourteenth which means you're not even twenty-one yet."

"My birthday is in two days, sir."

"Shut your damn mouth, boy. I didn't ask you to speak!"

Son of a bitch. As he was being reprimanded he glanced down at his sneakers, hoping this bullshit would be over with soon, so he could go back and party. Then he heard three ominous words.

"You're under arrest."

"His head jerked up. For what?"

"Put your hands behind your back, little fucker."

Ronald did not comply. "Are you fucking serious?"

"Place your hands behind your back. I'm not going to say it again."
He put back his night stick and placed his hands on his handcuffs.

"But—"

Officer Cooper opted to grab his gun, instead of grabbing the taser.

Intimidated, the kid backed away, then started running away from the officers.

They were in no mood to chase after him; Officer Cooper didn't even think twice. Under Headley's command, Cooper aimed and fired. His bullet struck Ronald in the head.

Officer Cooper was overwhelmed by a feeling of euphoria. He was on cloud nine as he put his gun back in the holster—after blowing on the tip of it.

"Great shot! Someone's been practicing," Headley said.

The women inside the house started to scream, while a select few came outside, camera phones rolling as they tried to get boisterous with the police for their lack of discretion.

"What the fuck? Somebody call an ambulance!" one man shouted, as he ran from the front door to Ronald's lifeless body.

One guy wearing a Black Lives Matter T-shirt stormed up to Cooper. "You pigs need to be hung for shooting unarmed civilians," he said with a shaking voice.

"I thought he reached for a gun," Officer Cooper said. His mischievous grin teased the man.

"That's what you motherfuckers always say."

He shrugged his shoulders. "That's my story, and I'm sticking to it."

CHAPTER 2

November 14, 2014

Robert was lying on his bedroom floor, bleeding profusely from bullet wounds, as the shooter stood over his six-foot-one, 205-pound frame, smiling complacently and aiming a pistol at his head.

"Please, don't kill me. I have a family," Robert begged.

The shooter did not seem the least bit concerned as he pulled the trigger.

His tossing and turning woke his wife, Linda. He began yelling for help in his sleep again.

She knew what was happening. Robert was having another bad dream in the middle of the night. This was the third night in a row it had happened.

She removed her sleep mask, then reached over to the night table and turned on the lamp.

"Honey, it's okay. Calm down. Take a deep breath," she said soothingly. She embraced him as well as she could; he was huge in comparison to her petite figure.

The dream felt surreal, so Robert placed his hands over his face to make sure it was unscathed. His fingers were wet; he was bleeding! He opened his eyes and pulled his hands away, only to realize that beads of sweat were covering his face. He took a deep breath of relief.

After finding his composure, he felt foolish. He was supposed to be the man of the house and make his family feel protected. Instead, here he was, terrified over a dream. His wife was his backbone; she was always there when he needed her.

"Do you feel better?" she asked.

He nodded his head and continued to lie in her arms. Once he gathered his bearings, he said, "It happened again. I'm sorry for waking you, honey." A sigh followed his words.

"It's okay, sweetheart," she said in a mellifluent tone. Then she leaned down and gave him a peck on his forehead with her full, soft lips.

She could feel his heart beat as she held him in her arms. She worried about him. Robert's bad dreams were occurring more frequently; this was the third night this week he'd dreamt of being assassinated.

The dreams had frightened her, causing her to double-check that the doors were locked at night before going to bed. Two weeks ago, they had received hate mail, threatening to kill the entire family. One line stood out: *You niggers will get what's coming to you.* And the previous week, on her morning jog, Linda had been sexually harassed by a group of white men who had threatened to do all types of sexually deviant things to her. Now she used the treadmill at her gym. Two nights ago, their garage door had been vandalized. Someone had spray-painted the word nigger and the directive go back to Africa where you belong. SWAT stickers had also been plastered to the garage door.

When the police had finally shown up, they'd treated Robert like a criminal. Some in law enforcement despised him. To them, he was the contemporary version of the late great Malcolm X, and the powers that be didn't need a force like him going against the grain and causing trouble.

Robert couldn't stop thinking about his dream. In it, he had become a victim. He had been ambushed in his own home. He wasn't the least bit surprised that the man who had assassinated him was part of law enforcement. He distinctly remembered the uniformed officer from his dream; his badge read 1015.

Robert did not think law enforcement as a whole was corrupt, but he believed there were bad apples that created negative energy in law enforcement.

He also believed that there were "good cops." But if a good cop stood by and watched a bad cop commit a crime without saying anything, was he still a good cop, or was he just as culpable? After all, their job was to "protect and serve."

Robert asked himself this question until it became redundant. In the end, he came up with the conclusion that law enforcement was a gang, just like the Crips and Bloods. They were just in a position to get away with their crimes the majority of the time, creating a travesty of justice for minorities.

"Are you sleep already, honey?" Linda asked.

"No, I can't stop thinking about the dream; it felt more real than the last one."

"Elaborate. What do you mean?"

"I just feel that my time is approaching," he said his words dark and full of foreboding.

"Stop that," she reprimanded him, her voice cutting through the despair. "You know I don't like when you talk like that. Stop being so pessimistic!"

"Keep your voice down, before you wake Darius." Darius was their nephew, but they had adopted him after his mother died of breast cancer, because his father was not stable enough to watch after him.

"Linda, I don't like to talk like this, but it's how I feel. I can't help how I feel."

"Maybe your dreams are trying to convey a message that you need to hire some new security."

"What's wrong with the security I have?"

"I told you before that I don't like the way Jacob looks at me. He watches my every move."

"Jacob is the head of security for events. He's been my best friend since kindergarten! He looks at everybody like that. And you know he is overly protective of me; he's been that way since we were children. That's why I felt that he would be ideal for the position."

She sighed. "I guess I can see why you hired him, honey."

"I promise that, as soon as we find a house that is suitable for me, you, and Darius, we will move."

"Good. Maybe you will sleep better at night. The threats have literally been hitting close to home, and I would hate to see something happen to you."

He shrugged. "Success breeds hatred; you know I receive hate mail at least once a week from various groups of people threatening to take my life."

Some drug dealers did not like the idea of Robert's campaign, because it interfered with their profits; they viewed him as they would a rival gang member. On the other hand, there were other gang members who embraced him and his words. They wanted to change their lives. They were just a seminar away from turning over a new leaf.

Then there were those who practiced white supremacy. They wanted him dead, simply because of the shade of his skin. The threats that these adversaries were making were starting to cause him and his family to lose sleep.

He shook his head. "You know it's all people, black and white, who hate to see me do what I do for our community. Drug dealers and corrupt police try to stunt our growth by keeping us from attaining certain achievements in life. And all I do is uplift the community."

"You can't please everyone, dear; you should know that by now."

Linda turned off the lamp. They shifted into a spoon position. Robert embraced his wife from behind.

"I'm sorry for waking you, honey."

"Don't be sorry. But now, you have to find a way to put me back to sleep."

It wasn't long before she felt something underneath the blanket poking her ample backside.

"Robert? Is that a flashlight, or are you happy to see me?"

"It's definitely not a flashlight," he said.

CHAPTER 3

The following morning, Leon stopped by his sister's house, under the guise that he wanted to wish his estranged son, Darius, a happy birthday. Linda and Robert had adopted Darius when he was just ten years of age. He was seventeen now. Linda had been best friends with Leon's wife. On Karen's deathbed, Linda had promised to watch after Darius.

Today was no different than any other day Leon decided to surface in his son's life—he had ulterior motives. He had lost a substantial amount of weight over the past couple of years, due to his heroin addiction, and like most times that he surfaced, he was only in need of a fix.

Leon, of course, couldn't get a fix at Linda's house, but he could make use of his propensity to steal, which was a step in the right direction. In the past, valuables had disappeared when he'd gone to the Carter's residence. After his last visit, Robert could not find his limited edition, Louis Armstrong, twelve-inch vinyl; since then, he hadn't been over. That was months ago. Leon was sure that Robert had forgotten about it by now. He didn't have a car anymore, because he had sold it to get high. His hair wasn't combed, and his fingernails weren't cut. His appearance was so unkempt, it made the homeless people in the neighborhood want to donate to him. Most women held on to their pocketbooks a little tighter whenever he walked near them. And they were smart to do so; snatching an old lady's purse was not beneath him.

As he walked up the driveway in his well-worn gray sweatpants and his tattered, camel-colored peacoat, he saw Darius outside with his puppy. Darius was autistic. It was best if he were supervised, because he couldn't be responsible for himself. In school, he stayed in one classroom all day, because he was in need of close monitoring; he liked to wander off.

Leon stood there for a moment and scratched his chin with his long nails, before deciding to speak. "Darius, what are you doing outside alone, hmm?" His saliva nearly hit Darius on the chin.

"Hi, Dad," the boy said in excitement with a broad smile. "I'm taking Buddy for a walk." Buddy was the three-month-old, light brown pit bull that Darius had gotten a month ago. Already, he had grown close to it.

Darius ran up to his father and wrapped his arms around him, playfully giving him a bear hug, lifting him off his feet. He was always glued in front of the television, watching professional wrestlers; he loved to emulate their every move. Standing at approximately six feet and weighing 235 pounds, he didn't know his own strength.

The hug was beginning to overwhelm Leon. He felt like he was going to pass out from the lack of oxygen. He tried to escape Darius's grip, but to no avail.

"That's enough, Darius, that's enough. I can't breathe. Let go!"

The boy finally let his father go.

He landed back on his feet, doubled over and started coughing. After catching his breath he began speaking again.

"Thank God! Darius, you know you should not be outside unsupervised."

"What does unsupervised mean?"

Given his size, people—Leon included—sometimes forgot that Darius had poor comprehension skills.

"You know that you shouldn't be out here alone, Darius," he rephrased.

"I can watch myself. I'm a big boy!"

Darius puffed out his chest with pride.

"You're a big boy, huh?"

Leon ruffled Darius's hair and smiled.

"Yes, Dad."

"Okay, then. Is your Aunt Linda awake?"

"I don't know," he said.

"I'm going to go check," Leon told him.

"Not so fast, Dad. Uncle Robert says he's tired of seeing your black ass because you always want money." Darius looked at him with the innocence of a child who didn't comprehend the full meaning of what he was saying.

Leon gave him a stern look. "Excuse me."

"Oops. I said a bad word."

Leon shook his head. "Darius, don't talk like that. It's not nice."

"But that's what Uncle Robert said!"

"Your Uncle Robert is a prick."

"Dad? What's a prick?"

His eyes narrowed. "It's your Uncle Robert's nickname."

At one point, Leon had not been allowed to stop by, because various things had ended up missing right after Leon had left their home.

Growing up, he'd been labeled a pickpocket and given the moniker sticky fingers. The title was well earned. Usually, he would be on the, NYC subway swindling people out of their valuables—mainly jewelry and wallets. He was even experienced enough to pull a wedding band off of a mark's finger without being noticed.

A career criminal, he had been in and out of juvenile detention centers since the age of seventeen. His mother had prayed that he would get his act together before it cost him his freedom permanently. When his mother succumbed to pneumonia, he lost his mind and began experimenting with hardcore drugs to numb the pain. That was the only way he could fill the void after her death. He loved her dearly. Without her, drugs were his solace.

As a boy, he had idolized Houdini. He had wanted to become a magician and had actually been great at magic tricks, but he'd started to lose interest once he formed the coke habit. After that, he spent all of his time chasing his high, and he began to use his sleight of hand techniques for evil.

Despite his actions, he and his sister had been close until she'd moved out and married Robert. It was a fact that Dr. Carter didn't care much for his brother-in-law; he had seen right through Leon and his shenanigans on day one. The two men had been feuding since high school, when Leon had allegedly stolen money from Robert. Since that day, the two men had been at odds.

Leon didn't like anyone to come between him and his little sister. She was all that he had left. He would literally kill for her.

"Linda," he called out.

"I'm in the kitchen, Leon."

Leon walked into the house and headed straight toward the kitchen. They gave each other a hug.

Once Leon pulled away, he didn't waste any time. "Hey, Linda. Do you have ten dollars that I can borrow?"

She was upset that he had asked her for money.

"No, I do not."

"Then what's this, hmm?" He opened his hand, producing the ten-dollar bill that had been in her pocket just before they'd embraced each other.

"Leon, give it back. I'm not giving you money to get high!"

"Keep your voice down, before Robert hears you." He put his finger over his lips. "I promise, it's not for getting high."

"Who do you think you're fooling? I'm your sister; I know when you are not being honest."

"Please, Linda," he begged, fingers interlocked.

"Leon, I love you too much to see you throw your life away."

He started scratching his neck, then his elbow—typical mannerisms of a dope fiend.

"It's not for drugs. I promise!" he lied, crossing his fingers behind his back.

Robert walked into the kitchen.

Leon suddenly switched gears. "Good morning, Robert. How are you?"

"I'm fine, Leon. What are you doing here?"

"I came by to wish my son a happy birthday." He smoothly slid his sister's ten-dollar bill into his pants pocket as he smiled, revealing a mouthful of teeth that would ruin most people's appetite.

"That's nice of you." He turned to Linda. "Suddenly, I'm not that hungry. I think I will skip breakfast." Robert said as he made himself a cup of coffee in his mug that read #1 Uncle.

Leon pulled out his phone and texted his drug dealer: BE THERE SHORTLY FOR MY DIME BAG. "Well, I'm in a bit of a rush. I just wanted to stop by to say hello."

Robert nodded, then said, "Linda, frisk your brother before he leaves."

Leon shook his head.

"You really don't like me, huh?"

"Well, ever since you stole my Louis Armstrong limited edition twelve-inch vinyl that I bought from an auction, I haven't thought much of you."

"How many times must I tell you that I didn't take it? Maybe you misplaced it!" Leon retorted, his voice rising.

Robert glared at Leon. His stern look silenced the room. "Lower your voice in my house, Leon."

Darius walked into the kitchen with buddy and reached into the cabinet to grab a box of Cinnamon Toast Crunch.

"You . . . you," Leon stammered. "You know what? I don't have to take this!" He turned to his sister. "Linda, I love you. See you later."

"Uncle Robert is a priiick, Uncle Robert is a priiick," Darius sang.

Robert and Linda were gapping at each other in befuddlement.

"Where did he learn that word?" Linda asked

"My dad taught me it this morning," Darius explained. "He said it was your nickname, Uncle Robert."

By the time Robert and Linda turned to look at Leon, he had vanished.

As he was leaving, Buddy followed him outside. Leon looked at the puppy and had an idea. "I bet I can make a couple dollars off of you, so you're coming with me. I know some Asian people that would love to meet you!"

After picking up the dog by its collar and shoving it under his coat he looked around to see if anyone had noticed. With no witnesses in sight, he walked up the block, whistling. This would allow him to get an even bigger fix.

CHAPTER 4

*L*eon reached the Chinese restaurant on Montauk Highway; the owner was just opening up.

"Leon! Long time, no see," the man said.

"I got something for you, Jackie." He held up Buddy.

As he envisioned food for his customers, the owner smiled broadly and told Leon to go around back. Buddy started barking and trying to wiggle himself free, but Leon held onto him tightly. His little nostrils flaring, the puppy could sense that something was not right.

"Everything is going to be alrighty, boy!" Leon said, in a failed attempt to pacify the puppy.

He walked to the back of the restaurant with Buddy in his arms, while intermittently looking over his shoulder, because he knew he was about to do something dishonorable.

"He's so cute, Jackie said once they were situated in the back room. He nearly started salivating; he couldn't wait to run his hands through the puppy's hair.

"I got this beautiful puppy for sale. Give me a hundred dollars, and he's yours," Leon said. The Asian man wiped his nose from the spittle Leon had delivered. Then he shook his head. "Leon, that's nasty. Why you always spit on me when we talk?"

"I'm sorry about that; I will give you a discount and only charge you ninety bucks."

The man noticed the way Leon was scratching himself. He also noticed the look of desperation in Leon's eyes. Such desperation could be used to his advantage. "You're crazy, Leon. I got fifteen."

"That must be your favorite quote, because you always offer me fifteen dollars, no matter what I bring to you."

The Asian man folded his arms over his chest and tapped his foot against the floor. From experience, he knew that Leon would rather walk away with fifteen dollars than walk away empty-handed. The Chinese restaurant up the road would pay him ten dollars.

Leon did not see any room to haggle; he needed his fix. "Okay. Deal."

When the Asian pulled out his wallet, Leon thought about snatching it and running, but it didn't look like much money was in there; it wasn't worth ruining their relationship.

"Thirteen, fourteen, fifteen. Here you go, that's most of the money I had inside my wallet. I only have two dollars left."

"Whatever, man. You are robbing me," Leon said as they made the exchange.

"Look who's talking!" The Asian man laughed and kissed the puppy on the forehead.

The puppy looked despondent, as if he knew what was to come. He could smell the death of his peers in the air. Their remains were sitting in the walk-in cooler, just a few feet away.

"You have a new best friend," Leon said to the man.

"I don't want to get too close with him, because eventually, I have to use him to feed my customers."

"You're sick, man." Leon stuck his tongue out in disgust.

"Pit bulls taste the best. My customers lick their fingers clean when I substitute them for beef."

"That's why I don't eat Chinese," Leon said as he shook his head.

"You're missing out." He glanced at the door to the dining room. "I must hurry, before my customers start arriving."

"See you later." He waved, walking away.

Buddy barked. Leon looked back, and for a split second, he thought about taking the puppy back. He knew Darius was probably looking all over for his puppy, but Leon's needs had to be met. It was no secret that his needs took precedence over everyone else's. He shrugged his shoulders and continued walking. The next stop was to his dealer.

"Sorry, little fella," he mumbled. A wave of guilt dissipated into nonexistence.

CHAPTER 5

*L*eon had already gotten high, but that had been during breakfast hours. Now, it was the afternoon, and he needed another fix in order to function.

He and his junkie girlfriend, Valerie, were desperate, but they had devised a plan to burglarize a house that they had ransacked on two other occasions.

They usually targeted houses in North Bellport. They did not want to pillage from anyone they knew or saw on a daily basis, because the chances were too great that they would run into the person they'd stolen from.

Valerie was desperately in need of a fix. She hadn't gotten high with Leon this morning. He had decided not to make her privy to the ten dollars he had gotten from Linda or the fifteen dollars he had gotten for Darius's puppy, so she'd had to do without. Once they were finished with this job, she could feed her addiction.

Each time they ransacked the pretentious-looking home, they surfaced with enough jewelry and cash to get high for days without having to commit another criminal act. They both had a high tolerance for their drug of choice, but their dependency had become increasingly worse; they needed to get high throughout the day. Her habit was so bad that her two-year-old daughter, Alicia, had recently been taken away from her by child protective services. She'd promised herself that she would stop getting high so she could gain custody over her daughter again, but it was easier said than done. Her drug of choice wasn't willing to give her back her life.

Today, neither one of them was thinking clearly, and they had become complacent about trespassing into people's homes. Their only goal was to get high. It was paramount to everything: family, friends, and even their dignity. Incarceration and chemical dependency programs were forms of "rehabilitation" that had proved to be ineffective for both of them. They had lost a lot of respect from members of the community; they had exhausted people, places, and things. Now, all they had was each other.

"Okay. It's showtime." Leon let himself into the house, after getting a key from under the welcome mat. As soon as he walked in, he opened his large black duffle bag. Soon, it would be filled with expensive things. "Okay, so you know the plan. Right, Valerie?"

"Of course I do, baby! We are a team," she said proudly, as she scratched her forearm. Her craving was starting to mount.

"You stay down here, and I will take the upstairs."

"Okay. I love you, baby."

"I love you, too." She looked like she was about to shed a tear.

"Is everything all right?" he asked, as he opened the refrigerator and grabbed a slice of pizza covered in anchovies and a can of cola.

"Yeah . . . I've just been thinking a lot lately."

He took a large bite of the pizza, then continued speaking. "Thinking about your daughter again, huh?"

She nodded her head.

"Okay. Tell me all about it later." He had another bite of pizza and continued upstairs.

He didn't really have any intention of listening to what she had to say, and she knew that. Leon was self-centered. Everybody who knew him was well aware of that fact.

As he got halfway up the stairs, he turned and saw that she was still staring at him. He suddenly had misgivings about what they were about to do. She was nineteen, and he was thirty-nine. He had gotten her involved in drugs, which had led to Alicia getting taken away. Oh well, he thought.

He was too callous to worry about it. He couldn't even remember the last selfless thing he had done.

She blew him a kiss.

He winked at her and continued up the stairs, drinking the cola as he went.

"He loves the drugs more than me," she said, watching him.

How had she gotten herself into this mess? She should have listened to her parents. Now they didn't want anything to do with her.

She took a deep breath, walked into the bathroom, and went straight toward the medicine cabinet. Spotting oxycotin and hydrocodone prescriptions, she grinned and threw them in her duffle bag.

After closing the medicine cabinet, she looked up, startled. She hadn't heard anyone enter the bathroom, but she was now face-to-face with a young lady.

The intruder had eyes that were as red as tomatoes, bags under her eyes from lack of sleep, and hair that might be housing small creatures.

Valerie let out a scream. So did the stranger

It only took her a moment to realize that the young lady looking back at her was really her reflection in the mirror.

It had been awhile since she'd last had the opportunity to see her reflection. Shame washed over her. She could not believe she had allowed herself to go this route.

The skin on her face was breaking out, her teeth were the shade of mustard, and her hair hadn't seen a comb in days. Her classmates would not believe she had let herself go like this. In high school, other female students had aspired to be like Valerie.

She began to shed tears. Her grandmother was probably rolling over in her grave at that very moment.

"I'm sorry that I failed you, grandmother." Right then, she had an epiphany. She began to put the painkillers back in the medicine cabinet and walk out of that house, leaving Leon behind and getting the help she needed. She wanted to get her daughter out of foster care.

She would be so proud to see her mother's reaction, once she got clean.

She walked out the bathroom and saw a large white man, standing in the hallway and pointing a rifle at her face.

"I was expecting you."

She closed her eyes and prayed, but her prayers weren't answered. The first shot killed her instantly. Her head shattered to nothingness after she was struck by the bullet. The only thing she was guaranteed now was a closed casket at her own funeral.

Leon heard the fatal shot from upstairs. Suddenly, he stopped stuffing his bag with valuables that didn't belong to him and started searching for an escape route. Leon opened the door nearest to him. The closet. He definitely wasn't going to hide in there. It was filled with correctional officer uniforms, in addition to several his-and-her tailored Ku Klux Klan uniforms.

"You're next, you black bastard. Do you think that you can come into my home and steal from me?" the homeowner shouted from the bottom of the staircase.

Leon wasn't about to go downstairs. He wasn't too concerned at all about what had happened to Valerie. With his bag of stolen goods in hand, he rushed over to the bedroom window, opened it, and jumped from the second floor.

He wasn't going to let the homeowner climb up the staircase and make him a casualty, like he had probably done to Valerie.

Once outside, he got inside Valerie's car and pulled away, without looking for oncoming traffic. He nearly hit an oncoming SUV with a mother and her three year old.

The women pulled over and said a prayer, then she immediately called her husband to tell him that she and their son had nearly collided with a reckless driver.

At the same moment, Leon was calling Valerie on her cell phone.

After he called several times and didn't get an answer, he knew he would never hear from her again. The first chance he got, he knew he had to pull over and say a prayer.

The man whose house had been robbed was a correctional officer named Thomas Mitchell. He was furious that he hadn't caught the second home invader. At his place of employment, he monitored the behavior of a number of young black men. Since he'd missed one here at the house, he'd make sure that the ones at work would feel his wrath.

CHAPTER 6

Congressman Kelly Boyd and Suffolk County District Attorney Jim Stroud sat at the bar at Henry's pub, after a long day on the job. The men were engaging in a conversation about Dr. Robert Carter.

"As the Italian mob would say, Dr. Robert Carter needs to be whacked! He is getting in the way," said the congressman, after he took a sip of his drink.

The district attorney only shook his head, as he nursed the drink in his hand before speaking. He had a thing for prosecuting young black men and a penchant for giving them harsh sentences. He hated them!

He had been traumatized at fifteen years old, when both his mother and father had been killed by a black man. The home invasion had changed his life forever, making him want to imprison as many black men as humanly possible.

"We definitely can't have that," the district attorney replied. "They must keep killing each other and calling each other niggers and bitches. For the past few months, black-on-black crime has declined thirty-five percent. Do you hear me? Thirty-five fucking percent. And that is not conducive to my rendering harsh sentences. Carter has to be eliminated." The district attorney's face began to turn beet red.

He finished his drink before continuing. "Oh, but don't worry. He will be taken care of. I have an officer that is literally crazy enough for the task. Everything will go according to plan. Unbeknownst to Robert, some of the people he works hand-in-hand with are good informants of mine. They blend in well, with their nappy heads, and they inform me about everything he discusses in their meetings.

"Hopefully, everything goes as planned, because he is far too intelligent for a black man, and we don't need more like him. We need them to continue to aspire to be drug dealers and to quote gangster rappers who hurl self-destructive lyrics to the ghettos of America."

"I concur," said the district attorney. "Plus, he has too much incriminating information on us, so it is imperative that he be forever silenced. He has helped put away a few good men, whom I have known over the years, and he has recently threatened to do it again, but we cannot allow that to happen. It will be messy, for sure."

The drinks were beginning to lower the men's inhibitions. They were slow on the uptake, and their need for discretion was quickly fading. Todd, the bartender, caught an earful of the malignant conversation the men were having.

"So, how's the wife," the district attorney asked, conveniently changing the topic once he noticed Todd walking toward their end of the bar.

"What?" he asked with a befuddled look.

He signaled to the congressman with his eyes.

"Oh, she's doing good. Thanks for asking."

From the snippets of conversation that he managed to hear, Todd knew the men were corrupt. But he was an Uncle Tom. He could care less about their discussion, as long as nothing that the men said had a direct effect on him. His wife was white, and so were his adopted children. As far as he was concerned, the young black men being shot and killed at the hands of the police did not concern him, even though he was the same shade as them.

"Can I get you gentlemen anything else?" he asked with a casual air.

"No, thank you, Todd." The district attorney reached for his wallet, pulled out two twenty-dollar bills, and placed them on the counter. One of the bills appeared to have blood on it.

Todd reached for the money, then hesitated.

The district attorney's money was just as dirty as he was. The dried blood on it was a testament to the corrupt life that he led.

"Speak of the devil," the district attorney said, as he looked up at the television screen and saw Dr. Carter.

"Todd, can you turn up the volume a little?" the congressman asked.

Todd turned up the volume and walked over to service another customer.

"I have the honor of interviewing Dr. Robert Carter tomorrow morning. He will be in our studios, live, tomorrow morning, to discuss a number of things, one of them being the corrupt judicial system in America. Tune in tomorrow morning at nine a.m. You don't want to miss it," the jubilant CNN journalist said.

"If he makes it to that interview tomorrow, he will expose a lot of people. This will be one of the biggest scandals in American history!" the congressman hissed.

"Too bad for him that he won't make it there. My cousin, Officer Cooper, will not allow that to happen," the district attorney said.

"So, what now?"

The district attorney glanced at his watch before speaking. Then he looked across the room and his eyes landed on a young prostitute and winked at a young lady. "It's still early, and I told my wife that I would be home late, so I have time to take Amy to a cheap motel and fuck her."

Amy was a local prostitute, She was always accessible for a good time—and so was every orifice on her body. For the right price, nothing was off-limits. The brunette stood up and followed him out to the parking lot. Then, they were off to the nearest motel.

CHAPTER 7

Robert was in the Boys and Girls Club building on Atlantic Avenue, where the community outreach program was held for underprivileged kids. He was on the phone, talking to his wife.

"Now, I'm beginning to worry. I can't believe that Buddy hasn't come back home by now," he said.

"Me too, honey. We are still looking. I got in my car and drove around the neighborhood, but no luck."

"I don't know why, but something tells me that your junkie brother had something to do with this." He tightened his grip on the phone.

"Calm down, Robert. Don't jump to conclusions! Maybe he just wandered off; he'll be back."

"We'll see. Put Darius on, would you?"

After a moment, he heard "Hi, Uncle."

"Hey, Darius. How are you?"

"I've been better. My classmates Joseph and Richard are here to keep me company until you arrive, but I miss my puppy."

"Well, later, when I get home, I will look for him. If we can't find him, Aunt Linda and I will get you another puppy."

"I don't want another puppy! I want my—"

"Okay, Darius. I understand." Robert noticed his friend and head of security Jacob, a tall black male, neatly dressed in a black tailored suit and black bow tie, walking toward him with a *Newsday* paper in hand. The man looked furious. Robert already knew what was on the front page of the newspaper: "Officer Not Charged for Killing African-American Party-Goer."

"Darius, tell Aunt Linda that I will call her back later. I love you."

"All right, Uncle Robert. I love you, too."

He hung up, just in time.

"Robert, have you seen this shit? This has to stop; these police are killing off the black youth at an alarming rate!"

"I have seen it, and it infuriates me. That boy's parents are staunch supporters of mine. We will expound on this and on other untimely deaths—not only police brutality, but black-on-black crime, as well. We, as black people, need to value each other. And as adults, we must lead by example."

"I couldn't agree with you more, my friend," Jacob said as he pat Dr. Carter on the back.

"I appreciate you, Jacob. The security that you and your team provide really helps to keep my events safe."

Jacob smiled. "That's what I'm here for, friend."

"Good. That's good. I'm ready to do this."

"It's a full house tonight. I see a few unfamiliar faces. All of my men are in place, just in case someone decides to try something."

Their open house was a highly anticipated event in the community. People started to take their seats.

Robert stood up in front of a room filled with his advocates. He knew he had influence over them. They listened to his every word and catered to his every whim. To some, he was like the father they'd never had. When he spoke, they listened intently and absorbed what he had to share.

Robert's agenda was to enlighten them, teach them etiquette, and make them cognizant of what was going on in the world. He didn't want them doing things that would potentially be harmful or land them in prison. He wanted to break the vicious cycle that seemed to be perpetuated in the urban community.

"Good evening, brothers and sisters." He gazed at a sea of camaraderie, filled with beautiful black faces.

"Good evening," the audience said in uniformity.

"I'm glad that you all could make it here tonight. We gather here to speak about the injustices that law enforcement continues to serve upon our community." He paused, then held up the same paper that Jacob had given him a moment ago. "This is proof that our community is under attack. We must fight back. Eric Garner was a victim! Mike Brown was a victim! Unfortunately, the list goes on. And now, this!" Robert shouted.

The crowd agreed, some in silence, some with nodding heads, and others with heated whispers. Ronald's mother held a tissue drenched in her tears of agony. Her husband placed his arm around her.

Preach, brother," an elderly lady in the front row said.

"A young man was killed at the hands of police recently. His parents are here. I send my condolences to them. They are taking donations to help with his memorial services. Robert shook his head. "This shouldn't have happened. The police are supposed to protect and serve our community, but instead, they are undermining us by imprisoning and murdering us, one by one, until our population is reduced, so they will feel comfortable enough to move in on us, like they did to our ancestors in Africa. History will repeat itself, and our job is to prevent this as much as we can. Solidarity is key, brothers and sisters."

He paused and looked around the room. "Our oppressors want to stop the positivity that I promote among my people. They despise camaraderie in the black community. Black-on-black crime put a smile on their face, but they frown when we unite, because it intimidates them. So, they lock us up. They set a high bail, and we get a disproportionate jail sentence for our crimes. These are facts. But we are at fault, too. We are not all innocent, which is why I want to talk to the Crips, and the Bloods."

Some gang members were present. In fact, the members with the most clout were in attendance. They were wearing designated colors—blue and others red—to represent their gang with pride.

"I want to ask the gang members a serious question. Why do you kill your brothers and sisters on a daily basis?"

A Blood gang member named Sniper, wearing a red bandana tied around his head, decided to speak. He even had the decency to raise his hand, because he respected Dr. Carter.

"I can answer that." He stood up and taunted the crowd with a smug look on his face.

Robert listened to his inner voice of reason and exercised some restraint. "Go right ahead, brother. State your name."

"My name is Sniper, but you can just call me Larry this evening. And to answer your question, we kill over territory, because if you're on my turf, selling to junkies, and you're not part of my crew, in my mind, you have a death wish."

"So you're willing to kill over your 'territory'?"

"Yes, sir. I cannot allow the next man to stand on my block and sell drugs to my customers," Larry said.

"You sound proud of that. But you were misguided, and you are perpetuating the cycle by misguiding the youth. We must try to break free of bad habits and not harbor them. Do you know how precious a life is?"

"I do."

He vehemently shook his head. "You can't possibly know, or else you would not do the devil's work for him by promoting such negativity! When gangs have shoot-outs, innocent people can potentially get shot and killed by stray bullets. Does that concern you?"

He pouted his lips, then looked around the room at the overwhelming number of angry black faces. Suddenly, his mounting defiance was reduced to a reasonable response.

"Maybe not in the heat of the moment, but I think about stuff like that."

"You're obviously not thinking hard enough, if you're continuing to do these things, black man. You are collaborating with the white man to destroy your own community. Is that something you are proud of?"

From a row behind him, a grieving mother decided to interject.

"You damn gang bangers are no better than these crooked cops! Allegedly, some gangsters did a drive-by on my seventeen-year-old son Curtis, in front of our house last summer. Police still haven't found the savages that killed my baby," one lady shouted from a row behind.

Embarrassed, the gangster looked around the room and saw some people shaking their heads in disgust. He suddenly wished he hadn't decided to speak. He shook his head. "No, sir, I'm not proud of my actions."

"Are you willing to change?"

He sat there, thinking about the hit that he had recently ordered on Rocket and wondering if it was worth it to carry it out. Especially now. What Dr. Carter had said made a lot of sense. He then stood up and looked around the room. He met the eyes of the leader of a rival gang, a formidable-looking man, with tattoo tear drops underneath his left eye, and a blue bandana tied around his head. Right now, it was more important that they became allies, instead of harboring resentment. He nodded and was countered with a nod from Rocket, the leader of the rival Crip gang.

"Yes. I am."

"Then let's end all of the senseless killings. It stops tonight. I demand a truce. In order to carry out my plan, we all must be in solidarity. You see, unity is one of their biggest fears. United we stand, divided we fall," Robert declared.

Then the community witnessed something that they never thought would happen in a million years. They were in awe when the leaders from each gang stood up, walked up to each other, and hugged. Only Robert could pull something like this together.

The audience gave them a standing ovation. Some even raised their fists in the air in a peaceful way. This marked a big day. Peace was near. "Congressman Kelly Boyd, Prosecutor Jim Stroud, Chief Daniel Murphy, and Officer Cooper are a few of the many people in a position of power who are on our list of the Ku Klux Klan members and associates." I plan to expose them tomorrow morning," Robert stated. The audience began to cheer and clap.

"We love you, Dr. Carter," the elderly lady in the front row shouted.

He waited until they'd settled down before he continued. "These men have caused so much grief in our communities. These men have been getting away with injustice. They have murdered and planted drugs on innocent black men for years!"

Robert had a list that revealed the corrupt law enforcement officers, judges, and district attorneys on Long Island. He was no stranger to justice. In the past, he revealed information that helped to prosecute corrupt law enforcement agents and politicians. So his was no idle threat; his words were to be taken seriously. He had actual proof, audio and video documentation, that revealed the corruption. He had received the footage anonymously and threatened to go public with it if things did not change and justice did not prevail. Someone was among the group that was a turncoat. He did not want to see Robert and his group of protégés prospers. In fact he was on the payroll of Officer Cooper.

An hour later, the meeting was over. Robert's security made sure that the building was empty and that everyone had made it to their cars safely before they were relieved of their duties. Back inside, Jacob went into a refrigerator and removed a cake.

"Robert, here is the cake that you asked me to pick up for you." Jacob handed him the cake.

"Darius's seventeenth birthday party is tonight. Are you coming to cut the cake?" Robert asked Jacob.

"I know I'm usually there, but not tonight. I'm far too exhausted. Tell Darius that I wish him a happy birthday."

CHAPTER 8

Officers Cooper and Headley had just left Spicy's restaurant and were sitting in their patrol car. Cooper was feeling ravenous, but Headley hadn't ordered anything, because he didn't have much of an appetite.

Today was the first day back for the officers, after three months of administrative leave with pay. The men had been partners for several years, but they were not only coworkers—they also lived together. They had a peculiar relationship. Officer Headley was Officer Cooper's shadow. The best friends confided in one another, especially about their white supremacy views, which played a major role in the chemistry they shared. They were one and the same; they spent so much time together that they even thought and talked alike.

Officer Cooper could not wait to have dinner. He was salivating over the smell of his fish sandwich and French fries. He opened a napkin, tucked it in his shirt, then took a bite so huge that he almost bit his finger. Then he spit the food out into a napkin. "Goddammit! I told that black bitch I didn't want any tomatoes on my sandwich, and she put them on here, anyway. I should shoot her in her big ass!"

"You want to shoot her over not making your sandwich correctly?" Headley asked.

"You and I both know I've shot and killed for less."

"Yeah, but you know brown people don't listen. They have low IQs."

"They're the worst race, those blacks—and those damn rice-and-bean-eating Puerto Ricans. Wastes of life. I'm about to go inside and give this waste of sperm a piece of my mind."

"Isn't your eighteen-year-old niece dating one of those tar babies?" Headley asked. He already knew the answer, but he wanted to add fuel to the already burning fire inside of Officer Cooper.

"Correction. She was dating a tar baby. Curtis didn't heed my warning when I told him to stop dating her. I followed Curtis black ass home one summer night, shot him in front of his house. I gave him his wings that night. Sent him to meet Emit Till. Newspapers called it 'gang related.' He'll never rear his nappy head again." Reliving the moment, he grinned.

"You are cold-blooded," Headley said with admiration.

"I'm only looking out for my niece's best interest. And doing God's work. She had just gotten a scholarship to Yale! I don't need her throwing her life away on a thug. He threw the food back into the brown bag and opened his car door, preparing to walk back into Spicy's. With one foot on the pavement, he turned and asked, "How come you don't ever drive?"

"It's best if you drive; trust me." Officer Headley winked.

"That's what you always say, lazy." Officer Cooper exited the car. Headley trailed behind him.

"You're not going to wait in line, are you?" Headley asked.

Suddenly, Officer Cooper didn't have the patience to wait in line like everyone else; instead, he walked up to the counter, where a customer was in the middle of placing an order, and interrupted, "Brittany, This fish sandwich is not the way I ordered it." He slammed the sandwich onto the counter, startling the worker.

The black male in the middle of placing his order was offended, but since it was Officer Cooper, he remained silent. He had seen too many white officers killing innocent black men and getting away scot free. And he knew that Officer Cooper was a rogue cop, so he decided not to speak his mind.

Officer Cooper's condescending attitude had upset the young lady, but she did not allow him to entice her. She was already one month behind on her rent, so the last thing she needed was to be terminated. It will not always be like this, she told herself. She aspired to be a registered nurse one day. She was eighteen and had a one-year-old daughter to take care of, so as much as she felt compelled to snap at the officer, she decided against it—especially once the image of her child, with no food to eat, flashed through her head.

She used all her willpower to be professional toward the officer, hoping that her supervisor would say something in her defense. But he was a coward. He acted as if he hadn't heard the officer, even though he was wiping down the counter within earshot. When she looked over at him, he conveniently walked away.

"What's that, Josh?" he called out, as he walked out of sight of the officer, pretending to have heard another employee call him.

She turned back to the officer. He looked familiar to her. She was sure she'd seen him somewhere before, but she could not figure it out. "I'm sorry, sir. What would you like?" she asked.

His eyes began to twitch. He wanted to slap her across the face the way he used to slap his estranged wife, Christine, when she would mess up his meal.

He rested his hand on his gun, as a form of intimidation.

At the sight of this not-so-subtle action, the previous customer lost his appetite. To him, his life was worth more than a burger and fries, so he left.

The employee, on the other hand, became furious. She'd recognized the man, once he'd placed his hand on the gun. The action triggered a depressing image that caused her to become emotional. She had a difficult time breathing. She told her co-worker, Gina, to complete the order. Then she walked to the back to grab her asthma pump. She'd recognized the officer as the one who'd shot her unarmed brother some months back. Timothy had left behind a wife and two kids.

Within minutes, Officer Cooper was given his order. He and Headley were on their way.

"Back to business," Officer Cooper said, sliding behind the wheel of his vehicle.

Then, his phone rang.

"Hello, Jacob," he answered.

He listened closely to Jacob's information. "Okay. Goodbye." Officer Cooper hung up.

"Is everything all right?" Headley asked.

"Yes. The meeting is over. His head of security just informed me that Dr. Carter is on his way home."

Headley rubbed his hands together in anticipation.

Just then, Robert Carter drove by; both men looked at each other and smiled.

They had worked together long enough to read each other's mind.

Carter was running on schedule. Their confidential informant was right.

"Take your gun off safety; we're going to have fun tonight."

"My gun is never on safety," Officer Cooper said.

Both men chuckled.

Officer Cooper turned on his siren and put his car in drive, in pursuit of Robert Carter.

CHAPTER 9

R obert was driving down Station Road when he heard a police siren, then noticed the flashing lights behind him. He decided to pull over on the shoulder of the road, so the police could go around him. Little did he know that he was the target.

When he pulled over, the police pulled up behind him. He did not know what was going on, but he remained calm and collected. He hadn't been speeding . . . maybe he had a broken tail light. Whatever the problem, he hoped it would be quickly remedied. All that was on his mind was going home and celebrating his nephew's seventeenth birthday.

"He's not going to know what hit him," Officer Cooper said.

Both officers exited their vehicle, grinning from ear to ear and engaging in light conversation as they walked toward Dr. Carter.

"His wife is fine, for a black woman. All I need is one night with her, and I will have that slut craving white cock," Officer Cooper joked. Both men laughed.

Officer Cooper approached the driver's side, and Headley approached the passenger side.

"Good evening, Officer," Robert said.

Officer Cooper deliberately ignored him and flashed his flashlight in Robert's face.

"License and registration."

Robert reached toward his glove compartment for his documents.

"Not so fast! Move nice and slow," Officer Cooper said, as both officers gripped the handles of their 9mm pistols.

To carry through with their malicious intentions, they wanted to provoke Robert. They were good at provoking black men; for them, it didn't take much.

Robert noticed Officer Cooper place his hand on his pistol through his peripheral vision. He began to sweat heavily. He knew he was being racially profiled and that the officer was trying to intimidate him, so he looked Officer Cooper in his eyes, then glanced down at his badge number, which was 1015! He was going to mention this incident in the morning during his interview, just in case the situation escalated.

Once the officer saw Robert looking at his badge, however, he took his hand and deliberately covered it.

By then Robert had already seen the numbers.

Robert just wanted to make it home safe to his family, so he complied, opening his glove compartment and reaching in, nice and slow.

"Are you trying to be funny, boy? We don't have all night," Officer Cooper shouted.

Who was he calling boy? It doesn't matter, Robert told himself. He realized that he wasn't in the position to be even a little aggressive, so he disregarded the comment and handed the officer his documents.

"Where are you coming from?" Officer Headley asked.

Robert didn't answer him.

"Are you deaf, dumb, or blind? I said, where are you coming from?"

"Officer Cooper, may I ask why I am being stopped?"

"You are just going to ignore my partner, smart ass?" Officer Cooper asked.

Robert looked around, but still failed to acknowledge Officer Headley.

"Officer, it's been a very long day. I'm tired, and I just want to go home to my family. So again, why am I being stopped?"

"Why are you being stopped? First of all, you don't ask the damn questions. We do, smart ass."

"Officer I didn't mean to be rude; I was just exercising my right and asking a simple question," Robert replied.

"Well, let me answer your question, sir," he said with abrasive sarcasm. "You are being stopped because you fit the description," Officer Cooper said. Both men chuckled.

What description? Being black? Robert was appalled. Officer Cooper could be out saving somebody's life, but instead, he chose to abuse his authority and harass him. "Excuse me?"

"Listen You fit the description of a man from a call we just received on our radio," the officer lied.

"I assure you that I did nothing wrong," he told Officer Cooper.

"That's what all you people say. But if you didn't do anything wrong, you have nothing to worry about."

Robert ground his teeth. "You are being very inappropriate, sir!"

Cooper's eyes narrowed.

"Inappropriate? You haven't seen me when I'm being inappropriate. Do me a favor and just sit there and close your goddam mouth, you big-lipped son of a bitch. Can you do that?"

Before Robert could respond, something in the back seat caught the officer's attention.

"What do we have here?"

"What are you talking about?"

He pointed to the birthday cake that Robert was bringing home for his Nephew. "Do you have any drugs in this cake?"

"That's inappropriate, sir."

"Answer the damn question."

"Of course not!"

"Well, you wouldn't mind if I check, now, would you?"

"Officer, it's my nephew's birthday cake, and I would like for him to receive it as is."

"I don't give a shit whose birthday it is. Now, pass it to me, or I will get it myself."

Robert did not say anything; he just shook his head in disbelief. The cake can be replaced, he thought to himself, as he retrieved the cake from the back seat and handed it to the officer.

"Happy 17th Birthday Darius," he read.

Robert just nodded.

"Sit tight. We'll be back," the officer sneered.

"What about my cake?"

Officer Cooper then did something spiteful. He intentionally dropped the cake on the ground, causing it to be ruined. "Oops," he said sarcastically, grinning.

The marble cake, covered in vanilla frosting, was on the ground.

Robert was upset, but he remained composed. He kept his hands on the steering wheel

The officers went back to their patrol car

When the officers went to their vehicle, they contrived a plan.

They walked back to Carter's vehicle and saw him reach for something. In the blink of an eye, both officers reached for their pistols and opened fire. Neighbors heard the gunshots and ran outside. The officers then reloaded the guns to squeeze a few more rounds at the man's motionless body—just in case he hadn't been dead already.

When they walked over to the car, they saw that in Robert's hand was a birthday card that read Happy 17th Birthday.

Officer Cooper called the chief of police, then waited for him to show up. He knew this would be a high-profile case, so he wanted to make sure that they didn't make any mistakes.

CHAPTER 10

*L*inda was jolted out of her sleep with a terrible migraine. She sat on the edge of her bed and used her palm to wipe the inordinate amount of perspiration from her forehead.

She'd just had a horrible dream that seemed so real. She'd witnessed Robert getting shot. There had been nothing she could do; she'd helplessly watched him pass away. Even now, fully awake, she was haunted by the horrific image of Robert, bleeding to death, as he cried out for help.

She got out of bed, walked to the top of the staircase, and called out, "Darius did your uncle get back yet?"

"He's not home yet, Aunt Linda," Darius replied.

She looked at her watch and began to worry. She grabbed her phone from the dresser and called him. His phone rang until it went to voicemail.

"Hello, honey. I just had a horrible dream, so I am calling to make sure that everything is okay. You know how I am. Call me back, okay? I love you."

She walked into her bathroom, opened the mirror over the sink, and took two Tylenol. After splashing cold water onto her face and drying off with a towel, she stood there, staring into the mirror at her pair of mesmerizing, large brown eyes.

She was exhausted from having worked all week. After that dream, she would not be able to go back to sleep until she heard her husband's voice.

She sat down on her bed and called him once more.

Many unsavory thoughts raced through her head, as Robert's agonizing scream continued to echo in her ears. A car accident, a robbery. Fearing the worst, she placed the phone to her ear. Her call went straight to voicemail. In all the time they had been together, that had never happened. He always made sure that his phone was charged, and he traveled with an extra battery, just in case of an emergency. He was meticulous like that.

Her heart began to beat even faster. Her migraine kicked against her skull. The voicemail was all the confirmation she needed. She knew in her heart that something was wrong. She placed the cordless phone back on the dresser.

If something had happened to him, she would lose her mind. He was her first love. He was her world. He was her strength.

They had been high school sweethearts in eleventh grade and inseparable ever since. It had taken him a while to approach her, because she hadn't been like all the other girls; she'd carried herself differently. She had been a stunning beauty, with her hair and nails always perfect and little need to wear makeup.

At first, she didn't know what to do; she was apprehensive about him, because of the company he kept. But once they got to know each other, they shared an amazing connection that not many couples experienced. They only had eyes for one another.

They were truly in love and had such a bond that being apart for more than a day, even now, would leave them in the doldrums.

With him by her side, she was content in life; she had a beautiful family and a wonderful house. What more could she ask for?

She was a hard worker, and so was he. They did everything in their power to provide for Darius, so he could live a better life than they'd had.

She tried calling him again. No answer.

At this point, worried was an understatement. She closed her eyes and took a deep breath. Then she heard a knock at her bedroom door.

"Aunt Linda?"

"Yes, Darius? Come in," she said.

Darius walked in with a birthday hat on and blew into a party horn.

Linda held her head and shut her eyes. "Darius, please. I have a migraine."

"I'm sorry, Aunt Linda."

She smiled slightly. "That's okay, Darius."

"Aunt Linda, my friends left at nine o'clock because they have to get up for school in the morning. When is Uncle Robert coming home?"

She glanced at the time.

"Hopefully, soon," she said.

CHAPTER 11

Chief of Police Daniel Murphy stepped out of his cruiser, took one last puff of his cigarette, and flicked it onto the cement. Then he lit another.

He walked toward Officer Cooper. Officer Headley's aloofness caused him to remain inside his car, because he disliked Chief Murphy and his nicotine habit. The chief didn't think much of Officer Headley, either. In fact, he never even acknowledged him.

"Are you all right?" he asked Cooper.

"Yes, Chief. I can't say the same for that guy, though." He nodded his head in the direction of Robert's lifeless body.

Coroners arrived at the scene and had Carter placed inside of a body bag and lifted onto a stretcher that would take him toward the coroner van.

"Hold on a minute, guys. Don't load him on there yet," the chief shouted.

He wanted to get a look at the corpse. Seeing a black man shot dead filled him with so much joy. Plus, he needed a good laugh, and he hadn't had one since he'd watched the movie Roots with his wife and kids a few days ago. His favorite part was when Kunta Kinte succumbed to the slave master and called himself Toby. He could relate to that scene, because he had made many young black men cry out in agony and beg endlessly for mercy, before he'd killed them.

He had the mentality of a slave master. His night stick was his whip. Chief Murphy had an aura that was condescending to black people. He hated them with a passion; he'd murdered and wrongfully imprisoned a significant number of blacks.

He stood in front of Carter's lifeless body on the stretcher. He unzipped the body bag; the sight of the man's body, riddled with bullets, nearly brought a smile to his face, right in front of the coroner. But he held it together. On the surface, he was professional enough to manage to look concerned, but the way he felt inwardly contradicted the masquerade of concern painted on his face. He stood there, stifling the urge to smile.

An angry crowd had already begun to form. One onlooker, a black man and former gang member, was devastated when he saw Robert's lifeless body. Even though seeing a fellow African-American murdered at the hand of a policeman was commonplace, this one hit close to home. This was their leader. Robert had been their last hope. Years ago, Dr. Carter had talked him into changing his life before it was too late. Now, in his absence, things would definitely take a turn for the worst.

"Why are you police so quick to shoot black people?" he asked from behind the yellow tape. He wiped the tears away from his eyes as his voice cracked.

"We shoot only when we feel our lives are in danger," Chief Murphy said.

"Dr. Carter ain't never hurt anyone. He was a positive man. He was an activist for human rights!"

"That's right," another person shouted.

"Son, we all have a dark side—even positive people. My officer said that he reached for a gun."

The angry man knew he would get nowhere talking like this to the chief, so he let his emotions get the best of him. He began chanting, "Fuck the police!"

The chief just shook his head. "Get them out of here," he ordered the other officers on the scene.

Once the chief had savored the sight of the corpse enough, he took a deep breath and covered the body back up. He had enough of a visual to go home later and mentally revisit the scene of the crime.

The nature of what had happened didn't faze him; his main concern was covering up for his department.

"Take it away," he said.

He then walked back over to Officer Cooper and looked over his shoulder to make sure he was not within earshot of the coroners. "Fuck him." He gestured with his chin toward the coroner van. "He's not my concern. My concerns are my officers that are out here risking their lives, day in and day out. Scum like him, with his Minister-Louis-Farrakhan viewpoint on life, makes our jobs harder. As far as I'm concerned, he got what was coming to him."

Chief Murphy walked up to Robert's car and opened the driver's side door, in order to inspect the vehicle before he concocted a story.

The first things he noticed were speckles of blood that covered the steering wheel and dashboard. Then he spotted brain fragments that nearly gave him a hard-on. In the coroner's haste to leave before the crowd got rowdy, they left the brain fragments behind.

The chief and Cooper sat inside the chief's car for privacy.

"Wow. How many times did he get popped?" The man was practically drooling.

"The bastard got shot up, Sean Bell style. What a rush! My adrenaline is through the roof. Woo!"

"I can see that, as clear as day. Do you have a story together yet?" the chief asked.

"Well, as we were approaching Mr. Carter's vehicle, he reached for something, while shouting, 'I'm going to kill you pigs.'"

"Excellent. That's all the defense you need: fear for your life. The law is on our side, not theirs. Remember that." After glancing over his shoulder again, Chief Murphy reached inside his pants pocket and handed the officer something—fairly routine behavior.

"This story needs to be sensationalized, so here is the cocaine that you can plant on him, as well. It gives him motive; he did not want to be taken into custody and have his reputation marred. Any questions?"

"Poker at my house or your house this Friday night?" Officer Cooper asked.

"Your house. My mother-in-law is coming over. I need a reason to get out of that damn house; that freaking lady drives me crazy."

Linda and Darius were sitting at the kitchen table, playing checkers as they waited for Robert. Linda had even tried calling Jacob, but she could not get through to him, either.

Darius raised his hands in the air in victory. "I won again, Aunt Linda," Darius shouted.

Linda took a deep breath. She wasn't wholeheartedly into the game, because her mind was occupied with thoughts about Robert.

"Can we play another game?" Darius asked.

She glanced at her wrist watch.

"Darius, that's enough for now. Get dressed, and let's go to the boys and girls club to look for your uncle."

"Okay."

Once Darius went to his room to get dressed, she heard a knock at the front door.

"Who is it?"

"Madeline."

She opened the door. Her neighbor had tears flowing down her face.

"Madeline, come in. What is it?"

"Please, have a seat, Linda. It's about Robert," she said.

Linda took a deep breath, then tears followed. Once she listened to the reason her close friend had come over, the pain was unparalleled to anything that she had ever felt. What was she going to do without her best friend?

A week later, they had Robert's memorial service. The funeral was full of people from all walks of life, people who all admired Dr. Robert. Even Leon showed up to help his sister with the grieving process.

PART 2

Black Angels

CHAPTER 12

February 16, 2015

Steven was a law-abiding citizen, but he was feeling jittery as he walked through the precinct doors on a brisk Monday morning. He was mentally exhausted, and the unsightly bags under his eyes were a telltale sign that he hadn't slept in days. He hadn't shaved lately, so the stubbles of grey facial hair stood out prominently, and he had on a black fedora and dark glasses, so his identity was kept secret—plus, the shades served as a shield to hide his enormous bags. What kept him up, what had his stomach churning, was the disturbing footage that he'd captured on his cell phone. Every time he closed his eyes, all he saw were the horrifying images of police brutality that he'd recorded. He had incriminating evidence of Officer Cooper assassinating Dr. Robert Carter.

As a white man, he had never experienced police brutality. His African-American brother-in-law, Greg, complained constantly about being pulled over and harassed for no reason. He kept thinking that Greg could just as easily have been Dr. Carter on that fatal night. Something had to be done. It had taken him awhile to muster his courage. But if Greg were a victim of injustice, he would want someone to speak on his behalf, if he could not.

Confident that his evidence would indict Officer Cooper on murder charges, he walked in and asked to speak to no one other than the honorable Officer Terrence. His brother in law told him that Officer

Terrence was the officer to trust with his evidence. A female officer at the front desk asked him to take a seat; within a few minutes, Officer Terrence appeared. He was surprised at how young the officer was.

Officer Terrence led the man into a small room, with two folding chairs on each side of a table and both men took a seat. Then Steven handed Officer Terrence a small yellow envelope.

"Officer Terrence, I choose to remain anonymous, out of fear of reprisal. I just wanted to personally make sure that you got this. I trust you will do what's right, young man."

"How do I get in contact with you?" the officer asked.

"Don't worry; I know where to find you," he replied.

Officer Terrence opened the yellow envelope and saw that a disc was inside.

After Steven left, he viewed it in private. He could not believe his eyes. More accurately, he didn't want to believe his eyes; it was a disheartening scene. Officer Terrence delivered the disk straight to the chief of police.

Chief Murphy appeared to be looking over work-related papers, but it was only a façade. In truth, he was absorbed in a pornographic magazine that he'd hidden.

Once he heard a knock on his door, he pulled his hand out of his pants, put the magazine in his desk drawer, and put on his reading glasses. Then he began looking over the pile of paperwork that he should have been reviewing in regard to police brutality. Now he looked the part.

"Come in," he said.

"Hey, Chief, can I have a word with you?" Officer Terrence asked.

"Depends on what it is that you want to discuss, son. I'm extremely busy today."

Terrence lowered his voice.

"It's in regard to Officer Cooper," he said.

The chief was looking at paperwork, then he raised his gaze and took his glasses off, placing them in front of him. Now the officer had his undivided attention. "Come in, son, and close the door behind you."

The young officer walked in, and the captain extended his hand for a handshake.

"Now, what is it that you want to tell me about Officer Cooper?" he asked, staring intently at the officer.

"I believe he is corrupt, sir."

"Corrupt! Now, son, that's a very serious accusation. What proof do you have?"

"I have footage that was given to me from someone who wishes to remain anonymous."

"Is that right." It was a statement, not a question.

"Yeah. It shows him murdering Dr. Robert Carter." He handed him the disc. "I didn't tell anyone yet, because I'm one hundred percent sure this will incite a riot."

"You're absolutely right; this information would surely cause a riot. So, this person that you speak of, he—or she—just randomly walked up to you and gave you this footage. He didn't leave his name, address, or a number where he could be reached, by any chance?"

The young black officer did not like the chief's response; his disappointment was clearly reflected in his facial expression. The chief seemed more interested in covering up for Cooper than following the oath he had taken.

"Sir, with all due respect, I just told you that Officer Cooper murdered someone. And that's all you have to say?"

The chief's eyes began to narrow.

"Listen, you little n-," he said, catching himself before the racial slur could be expressed completely.

The young officer's hands began curling into fists.

"Little what?" he snarled.

"Do you want to keep your job? I'm well connected. If you don't follow my orders, I will see to it that nobody hires you, because you're not being a team player," the chief said.

"Are you threatening me?" the officer asked.

"You're damn right, I'm threatening you. Is this the only copy you got?" the chief asked, holding up the recording.

"Please, tell me you're joking."

"This is no joke, son. Around here, we stick together, just like they do out there," he said. "Whose side are you on, anyway?" he growled.

"I'm on the side that is supposed to protect and serve the community. It's too bad we're not on the same team."

He paused for a moment, eyeing the officer shrewdly. "How are your parents? You have such wonderful parents. I would hate to see anything happen to them."

Officer Terrence flipped the chief his middle finger, then he stormed out, slamming the door behind him.

"He has to go," Chief Murphy said to himself. Then he picked up the phone and dialed a number that he only used when he was in need of a big favor.

"We need to talk," he said, as soon as the line connected. "I have an officer by the name of Aaron Terrence that wants to protect and serve the community. He seems like the type to potentially thwart my plans."

Cooper was thrilled. To him, this was great news. An opportunity to kill an African-American was an offer that he could never refuse. He was an advocate of population control of minorities. The only time that he smiled at a black person was when he saw him or her inside a coffin.

"I will take care of it," the cold voice on the other end of the phone said.

That night, Officer Terrence went to sleep; he would never wake up again.

CHAPTER 13

The following day, Officer Cooper walked inside the precinct in a jubilant mood. Newspaper in hand, he sauntered toward Chief Murphy's office. The headlines thrilled him; he'd hardly stopped grinning since he'd first picked up the paper. The article, in bold letters, was titled "OFFICER SLAIN DURING HOME INVASION."

Officer Cooper knocked on Chief Murphy's door.

"Come in," Chief Murphy said.

"Good morning, Chief," he practically sang as he opened the door.

"Good morning, Cooper."

Officer Cooper strolled into Chief Murphy's office and threw the paper on the top of his desk with a smirk.

The headline brought a matching smile to Chief Murphy's face. "That was fast," he said.

"It needed to be taken care of, before word got out. Word on the street is that other members from Carter's organization are about to pick up where he left off and do an interview exposing corrupt agents, judges, and politicians."

"Would you be so kind as to eradicate any other activist that is cut from the same cloth as Carter? Anyone that poses a potential threat?"

"I've been watching a few gang members that recently decided to turn over new leaves and become activists. I'm already on it," Officer Cooper said confidently, as he swaggered out the office, whistling.

Officer Cooper pulled in front of a small house. He felt a little nervous, sitting in his patrol car. Seldom was he apprehensive, but he did not know what to expect. The last time that he'd shown up unannounced, it hadn't ended well—a restraining order had been issued against him. But he got away with so much injustice toward citizens that he thought he was above the law; a restraining order wasn't going to stop him. He turned off his engine and sat there, staring at the house. The scene looked tranquil. He wanted to be a part of it. This time, he genuinely wanted to make the relationship work. He missed his family. He hadn't seen them in several months, due to his abusive nature toward his ex-wife and the questionable relationship that he shared with Officer Headley.

"I take it she's not expecting you—again," Officer Headley said.

"No, she's not expecting me. But I will never let her go," he replied.

Officer Cooper's sentiment was one-sided, because the lady that he was referring to was his estranged wife, and she had become almost oblivious to his existence.

After a few minutes, a yellow school bus pulled up at the end of the block. Two children got off and walked toward the house that he was waiting in front of.

"There they are, running right on schedule," Officer Cooper said.

"They've gotten big, how old are they now?" Headley asked.

"Eight and nine."

"Good luck this time." Officer Headley pat him on the back.

"Thanks. I'm going to be needing it. This is the longest we ever went without seeing each other." He hesitated, then took a deep breath and stepped out of the car.

His children saw him and ran down the sidewalk to him. His son reached him first, so Cooper gave him a big hug. Then his daughter ran over, and he embraced her, too. It felt great to be with his kids again. It had been awhile since he'd held them so close. For months, he'd wished he could tuck them in at night.

"Dad, what are you doing here? Are you and mom back together?", Christopher asked.

Then he provided his standard line: "We will always be together, even when we are apart."

"Dad, I missed you!", Samantha said.

"I missed you, too, sweetheart."

"Promise me you'll never leave," she demanded.

"Well, that's what I'm getting ready to talk to your mother about right now."

He held their hands as they walked up to the front door and let themselves in.

"Mom! Dad is here," Christopher shouted.

She was in the kitchen, prepping dinner. In the middle of slicing squash, she almost severed her finger when her son shouted that her ex-husband had shown up, uninvited. Again.

She sprinted to the front door and grabbed her children, as if they were in harm's way—as if they were talking to a stranger. To her, he had lost his identity and had, essentially, become a stranger—she no longer knew who he was. In the beginning, things had been fine, because he'd been able to hide who he really was from her, but once she'd seen his dark side, she'd begun to distance herself and the kids. The quintessential man, her knight in shining armor, had just been just a facade. Then, she'd learned of his corrupt ways and his hatred toward black people. Once he started controlling her and abusing her, she filed for divorce and an order of protection.

"Honey, I'm home," he said, as he stepped inside.

"You stay away from me," she snarled, backing away from him.

She continued to walk backwards, while keeping her eyes on him. Her hands started to tremble on Chris's and Samantha's shoulders.

He enjoyed seeing that the fear he'd instilled in her once upon a time was still active. "You don't miss me?"

She recognized the same psychotic look that he'd always had right before he'd wrap his hands around her neck and shake her violently. "Kids, go to your room," she demanded.

She didn't have to tell them twice. Instinctively, they ran to their room and hid under their bunkbed.

Once they were out of sight, she continued. "You are not allowed to be here. What do you want?"

He shrugged. "I just want to see my kids."

"You're far too abusive."

His eyes narrowed. "I'm better now. I promise."

But she could see, instantly, that he was not well. He had a deranged, look in his eyes.

She was done talking to him. His eyes were beginning to twitch, and the deranged look on his face was beginning to really make her uncomfortable. In the past, that had been a harbinger of domestic abuse. He was going to punch her at any minute.

Seemingly out of nowhere, Headley surfaced. "Smack that bitch," he instigated.

"Please, leave," she asked in a voice that trembled.

"I'm not leaving without my wife!" He grabbed her by the wrist.

"You're delusional! I'm no longer your wife, so let go of me!" she shouted.

Her father, a retired Marine, came out, toting a 12-gauge shotgun. "Get off this property, before things escalate," he calmly advised.

He let go of her wrist and took a step back. "I just came to see my family—"

"If you and your split personality don't get out of here, you're going to leave in a body bag." He cocked the gun.

It finally hit Officer Cooper: he had lost his grip on reality. His ex-wife's words reverberated in his head: "You're delusional!"

Momentarily, he saw things for what they were. His alter-ego, Officer Headley, was nonexistent. People didn't acknowledge Headley because the man only existed in Officer Cooper's subconscious mind.

CHAPTER 14

Linda had called out of work sick this morning. She finally decided to get out of bed. She noticed several missed calls. Some of her close colleagues, beginning to worry about her, had called to check on her.

She sat up and realized that she'd fallen asleep without eating again. The eggplant parmigiana from last night was sitting on her night table, where Madeline had left it. She didn't have much of an appetite these days. She was losing weight from not eating. Even her underwear wasn't as form-fitting as it had once been

I have to eat something, she thought to herself.

Devastated about her husband's passing, she didn't take pride in her appearance like she once had. Nowadays, she often looked disheveled. She no longer wore makeup, and she didn't get manicures or pedicures. Even her armpits and legs were badly in need of a razor. She simply was not motivated to look beautiful anymore.

After catching wind of Robert's death, some of her opportunistic male colleagues had made passes toward her, but she had spurned their advances. Her heart still belonged to Robert, and no other man could ever fill his shoes.

She did not know how she could continue living without her husband.

Parched, she reached for a nearly empty bottle of vodka and took a swig. She had been drinking so much lately that a small amount of the alcohol didn't have the same effect anymore.

She looked over on the table beside her bed, at the wedding photo of her and her late husband. He looked so handsome. She'd give anything just to see him once more, just to feel his touch. She missed the feel of his lips pressed passionately against hers.

She took a deep breath and sat on the edge of her bed. Then she took another swig of the vodka to finish it off.

Why had this happened to her?

She seldom left her bedroom anymore, not even to eat. She had become impervious to people and events since the passing of her husband. Her heart was aching.

She stood up, walked over to her dresser, and picked up a pen. Finally, she had the courage to begin writing the suicide note that she had been contemplating for the past few days. She kept it short and sweet.

February 17, 2015

Dear Madeline,

I tried my best, but I cannot seem to carry on like this. I realize that a piece of me has died along with Robert. I wish I could find the strength to continue, but—I'm sorry— unfortunately, I cannot. Make me proud, and please, watch over Darius. I just want to be reacquainted with the love of my life.

Love,

Linda

After she was done, she opened the dresser drawer and reached for a .357 magnum revolver. The gun was already loaded, because she'd attempted to take her life a few days prior, but she had experienced a change of heart at the last minute.

Now, as she stood there, tears began to surface in her eyes. She held the gun to the side of her head and closed her eyes.

Then she pulled the trigger.

Click.

"Dammit," she shouted.

For the second time in a row, she had failed to kill herself. There was only one bullet in the magnum revolver; she was playing a game of Russian roulette.

She heard a knock at her door.

"Aunt Linda, are you awake?" Darius asked.

She glanced at the alarm clock on her night table, then did a double take. School had let out an hour ago.

She took another deep breath and cleared her throat before speaking, in order to disguise her pain.

"Yes, honey. Is everything all right?"

She put the pistol away in her drawer and wiped the tears off her face, before opening the door.

"Yes, Aunt Linda. I have good news."

She hadn't heard him this excited in months. He had taken Robert's death hard.

"What is it, Darius?" She gave him a hug.

"My friend from school invited me to a sleepover on Friday! Can I go, Aunt Linda? Please?"

"Once I talk to his mother," she said.

Darius frowned at the sight of a stray tear.

"Thank you, Aunt Linda. Is everything all right?"

"Yes, dear. Everything is fine now." She looked into his eyes, then gave him another hug. She could not believe she had been about to commit suicide, leaving behind her nephew to fend for himself.

Darius was excited about his first sleepover, at Kenny's house.

Since it was in his nature to wander off, Linda was a little apprehensive about sending him to the sleepover. She was happy that he had made new friends in school, though. Lately, she had been encouraging him to be more social. He certainly was doing that!

CHAPTER 15

February 20, 2015

On the day of the sleepover, she dialed the number to Kenny's house and spoke to his mother, Connie.

"My name is Linda, and my son Darius was invited to Kenny's sleepover tonight," she explained.

"Oh, wonderful. How are you?"

On the brink of suicide. "I'm okay. Thanks for asking. I just wanted to go over a few things before I have my son sleep over, because Darius has special needs."

"Oh, I see. I recall Kenny mentioning that to me, but he didn't tell me what his disability was."

"Well, Darius has autism, and he is prone to wander off. That's why he has to be monitored and stay in one classroom for the entire day."

"Okay. I'm glad that you called and explained that to me. I will keep a close eye on him."

"That's wonderful! I'm so relieved, Connie."

"He is going to have such a great time; I promise. But you need my address. Do you have a pen, Linda?"

"This is my cell phone. Can you text it to me?"

The woman's air of responsibility caused Linda's uncertainty to vanish. In fact, it put a smile on Linda's face to know that, in her absence, Darius would be in good hands. If something happened to him, too, she wouldn't be able to bear it.

Linda pulled up to the address on Pearl Street, in North Bellport. After parking the car, she stared at the house in awe. It was a very large, imposing white house, located on the affluent side of town. She had never had much reason to go on that side of town. Kenny and his mother were standing outside, smiling and waving at them.

Darius was the first of four kids to arrive. He was so ecstatic that he had gotten an invitation to his first sleepover—with the most popular kids in his school—that he had shown up a half hour early.

Linda took a deep breath and put on a contrived smile as she got out of the car.

Kenny and his mother walked over to them. "Hi there! Did you guys have any trouble finding my place?"

"No, we found it easily," Linda said. "Thank God for GPS; I don't know what I would do without it!"

"Same here. Well, it is nice to finally meet you in person, Linda. This is my son, Kenny," Connie said. She stood behind her son with her hands on his shoulders, like a proud mother.

"Hey there, young man," Linda said. She shook hands with the preppy-dressed teenager.

"My name is Darius," Darius told Kenny's mother.

"Nice to meet you, Darius. You can call me Mrs. Schmidt. Okay?"

"Okay." He smiled.

Linda instantly realized that he had a crush on Kenny's mother. He had always been enamored with white women. She watched as saliva appeared at the corners of his mouth. Turning Darius toward the car, she wiped his mouth quickly. Thank God, she'd acted fast. No one had noticed.

"Kenny, help Darius with his bags," Connie said.

"Okay, Mom. Darius, how are you, man?" Kenny asked.

"I'm fine. How are you, Kenny?"

"I'm fine, too. Let me get your bag for you."

"Thank you, Kenny." Darius handed Kenny his sleeping bag.

As the two boys walked away, their mothers smiled.

"I wanted to ask you a question, Linda," Connie said.

"Yes? Go ahead."

"Besides Darius wandering off, is there anything else that I need to keep an eye out for? Does he have any allergic reactions, for example?"

"No, that's really it."

Darius came running out of the house, shouting, "Mom! They have a big screen TV!"

"That's wonderful, honey, but don't watch too much television. Don't forget that you have friends to talk to."

"He is a bit of a couch potato at home," Linda explained to Connie.

She smiled. "What is your favorite thing to watch on television, Darius?"

Darius smiled broadly.

"I like to watch wrestling. Right, Mom?"

"Yes, Darius." She smiled at Connie, then gave Darius a hug and a kiss on the forehead. "Behave yourself okay?"

"Yes, Aunt Linda."

"It was a pleasure meeting you, Connie." She leaned in for a quick hug.

"The pleasure was all mine," Connie replied.

As Linda was walking toward her car, she noticed a white man in his late thirties, standing on his front porch and staring at her with blatant hostility. Such evil was emanating from him as he ogled her that it almost made her change her mind about having Darius sleep over; but she didn't want to upset him. He had been looking forward to this sleepover all week. Maybe she was overreacting.

She decided to be cordial. As she drove by, she waved at him; he didn't even flinch.

Unbeknownst to Linda, he was a bigot. His prejudice didn't permit him to wave back to an African-American. As she drove by, he mouthed the word nigger.

Linda had already turned her head, though, so she hadn't caught him mouthing the racial epithet. If she had caught him, she would have gone right back to pick up Darius.

Noticing her introverted neighbor outside, Connie rushed Darius into the house. To her knowledge, her neighbor worked at a detention center for youths and had recently had his house burglarized by some dope fiends. The male was still at large, but her neighbor had killed a young woman in the process. The belligerent look he had in his eyes as he'd stared at Darius frightened her. She actually considered taking Darius home, but she knew he wanted to have some fun hanging out with his friends, so she decided to let him enjoy himself. Maybe she was overreacting.

CHAPTER 16

$\mathcal{I}$t was almost closing time at Henry's Pub. Officer Cooper was off from work today, and had been drinking an immoderate amount of alcohol. The more he drank, the more he felt consumed by guilt. It was his fault that his wife had taken the kids and left. This time, when she said that she was done, it seemed she really meant it. She was family-oriented, so it probably wouldn't work now, anyway, especially since her father was privy to the abuse. That guy had even pulled a gun on him! Maybe Cooper's relationship with his ex-wife had run its course.

The sound of an eight ball being knocked into the hole at a nearby pool table interrupted his pity party. His thoughts shifted as he took a look around the bar for the umpteenth time that night. He had grown paranoid over the years, especially because he had done a lot of harm to innocent people. Tonight, he felt like he was being watched.

Truth be told, he was being watched. Two opportunists had their eyes on him, as he continued to drown in his sorrows.

"Henry, let me get another drink," he ordered the bartender.

"Make that two, Henry." Amy, the local prostitute, walked over and sat next to Officer Cooper, placing her hand seductively on his back.

"What the—" Officer Cooper's words were cut off mid-sentence when he looked up to see who was touching him.

"Good evening," she said, gazing into his eyes flirtatiously.

He smiled.

She had been watching him ever since he'd walked into the bar, looking away only to apply her make-up a few minutes before joining him. From where she'd sat, she'd even been able to count how many drinks he'd consumed that night.

Thinking with his dick, he said, "What's your name, beautiful?" He stared at her exposed cleavage. His erection was starting to take shape in his jeans.

"Call me the lady of the evening," she said, as she placed her hand on his inner thigh. It was the same move she had made with many helpless men.

She noticed how inebriated he was and flashed a smile of her own. She liked her men drunk; they were more generous. She was only twenty-six, and already a veteran in her line of work. She had begun selling herself at seventeen, when she'd run away from home to be with her boyfriend. Later, her boyfriend had turned into her pimp.

Her hand moved to his crotch, while her other hand roamed freely over his arms, thighs, and buttocks. She was a freak.

The bartender took notice. Henry was a middle-aged man with a wife and kids. He would hate for anyone to sit by and watch another person take advantage of his loved ones. He would also despise a bartender who continued to pass people drinks beyond their point of being able to drive home safely. He decided to use his discretion and cut Officer Cooper off.

As he was drying out a beer mug with a towel, he took another look at the young lady trying to hustle Officer Cooper and decided to intervene. Even though word around town was that Officer Cooper had been involved with Robert's death, he believed in karma; if something happened to Officer Cooper on his watch, he would feel awful. He walked over, grabbed Officer Cooper's car keys off the counter, and placed them behind the bar. "Amy, how many times do I have to tell you to stay out of here?"

"Hey! Give me my keys back," Officer Cooper shouted.

"Pass me your wallet, too. You have to get a ride home; I will call you a taxi."

Henry wanted to save officer Cooper from Amy.

The young prostitute glared at Henry for thwarting her plans. She removed herself from the bar and walked away swiftly. She approached a black male who was playing pool. He had on a black leather jacket and blue jeans. His gold chain glinted in the dim light, as did several rings on his fingers. The man shot a cold stare at the bartender, and then signaled for the prostitute to leave with him. She grabbed her coat off a nearby chair and put it on. He wrapped his hand around her shoulder, and they quietly walked out of the bar together. Once she was outside, she handed him a wallet and an Iphone. He smiled.

"You're smooth, baby. I saw you take the phone within the first ten seconds, but not the wallet. I see you're getting adroit."

She'd almost gotten around to stealing his gun, too, but she'd been interrupted by the bartender.

"Thank you, baby. I learned from the best. Can we grab something to eat now?" she asked her pimp.

Because he was a penny-pincher, he took a few seconds to think about her request.

He'd known the girl for years. A friend had brought her to him, because she'd seen potential in the kid. So had he. Ever since that night, she'd been making him no less than a thousand a night—every night. The men that sought her services knew she was great. Some men traveled from different states, just for an hour of her time.

"You worked hard tonight, so dinner is on me," he said.

She smiled. "Thank you."

"You're welcome," he said, taking the credit, even though he knew that her intimacy with strangers was really paying for dinner.

"Give me a kiss," she demanded.

He gave her his hand to kiss, because he did not kiss his women on the mouth. To him, it was forbidden. Her mouth was his money-maker, and he'd witnessed her do very nasty things with his money-maker. Earlier that evening, before setting her eyes on Cooper, she had given a man a blow job for twenty bucks. So, she gave him a peck on the brown of his hand, and they held hands as they walked merrily to the first diner they came across.

Outside of the physical abuse, she was content with how he treated her. He loved her like no other man ever had. In her warped mind, a black eye here and there was just his way of showing that he loved her.

Back inside the bar, Cooper realized that Amy had stolen his phone and wallet but he was too drunk to really care. Henry knew that the duo would be long gone already, but if he ever bumped into them again, they would be sorry for having come into his establishment and stolen from his customers.

"Those two degenerates are not allowed back in here, Justin. If they come back, I will call the cops and have them arrested," he said to his nephew.

"I got it, Uncle Henry."

He glanced at Officer Cooper, who was sitting at the bar, his head on the counter. "Justin, I need you to close tonight. I'm going home early. I just have to use the restroom."

"Okay, Uncle Henry."

"I will be right back, Cooper." Henry gave him a pat on the shoulder as he walked by.

Officer Cooper picked his head up and waited until Henry had walked into the restroom. Then he walked behind the bar. He was after his keys, but Henry's nephew stood in front of him.

"I can't allow you to have your keys, sir."

"Little punk, if you don't get out of my way, you will be sorry." Officer Cooper reached for his service weapon.

That was enough for Justin to give in.

"Take your keys. Just don't shoot me!"

After the kid handed them over, Officer Cooper stormed out of the bar and got behind the wheel of his Toyota Camry.

It was a recipe for disaster.

Ten minutes later, Brittany, the cashier from Spicy's restaurant who's brother was murdered by Officer Cooper, came across a car accident on an unfrequented road. She stopped her car immediately.

The totaled car had crashed into a utility pole. As she stepped out of her car to help, she dialed 911 and ran up to the totaled vehicle. She prayed that the driver was still alive. Then, she heard the moans.

She had just left her internship for the day, so she still had on her nursing attire.

The victim was conscious. He felt a wave of relief, once he saw that that a medical professional was on site. "Please, help me," Officer Cooper said. He held out his hand to the nurse whom he'd met once before, under very different circumstances.

The woman recognized him. This was the cop that had killed her brother and come into her place of employment to humiliate her. "Nine-one-one. What's your emergency?" the operator asked.

The young lady stood there, in shock. But she didn't have much time to waste. Time was not on the officer's side.

She could see that he hadn't been wearing a seat belt and that he was losing a lot of blood.

"Please, help," he gasped. Again, he reached his hand out to her. It was the first time in his entire life that he felt happy to see a black face.

"Nine-one-one. What's your emergency?" the operator repeated. Then she heard a dial tone.

As the woman took a few steps back, Officer Cooper's vision started to grow dim. Then his vision faded to black. Seconds later, he heard a car door slam shut.

At that moment, he wished he could apologize to her. His last sight was of that young lady.

Once behind the wheel, she put her car in drive and stepped on the gas, leaving Officer Cooper to die a slow death.

Karma had finally caught up to Officer Cooper.

By the time his body was discovered, it was too late.

*L*ater that night, the boys were down in the basement, socializing. Two other boys, Michael and Shawn, had shown up after Darius, and another boy was supposed to arrive any minute. Darius was the only black kid in the room, but he didn't feel uncomfortable.

They heard a light knock on the basement door.

"You boys have another visitor," Connie said.

She came walking down the stairs with Joseph Taylor, the heartthrob captain of the Bellport High School football team. He was the most popular student at their school. Along with a bad temper, he had broad shoulders and huge biceps that served to give credence to the rumor that he used steroids. He practically had to turn sideways to fit through the basement door. Connie wasn't feeling too well, and it showed on her face. She felt congested, and her nose was running. She was going downstairs with Joseph just to say goodnight to the boys; then, she'd get some rest herself.

After greeting Joe, Kenny said, "Um, Mom? You don't look so well."

She sneezed, then used the napkin in her hand to wipe her nose.

"Bless you!" Michael and Shawn said in unison.

"Thank you, boys. I'm not feeling so good, but before I go upstairs to get some rest, I wanted to say goodnight."

"Goodnight," all the boys said.

Kenny's mother reciprocated with a smile, then walked back upstairs, closing the door behind her.

"Your mom is sexy, even when she looks sick," Joseph Taylor said.

"Hey! Watch your mouth," Kenny snapped.

Michael laughed. He was Joseph Taylor's sycophant, so he found anything that he said amusing.

"That's not nice," Darius commented.

"That's not nice," Joseph mimicked him. "Kenny, why did you invite this guy?"

"It's my birthday, so I invite who I want to invite," he said.

Kenny's parents had always taught him the importance of anti-bullying. He knew that bullying could lead to suicide or to a massacre on school grounds. So, recently, when another student had bullied Darius, Kenny had intervened. It was just the right thing to do.

"Calm your nerves. Listen, Kenny, I'm sorry about what I said about your mother. I got something that will help you to loosen up." Joseph pulled out a ziplock bag with half a pound of pungent-smelling marijuana.

"Let's get this party started!" his sidekick, Michael, said, as he rubbed his hands together.

Darius blinked in disbelief. "Mom told me to say no to drugs," he said.

"My mom told me the same thing, but did I listen? No!" Joseph grinned, while holding the bag of marijuana.

"I didn't listen, either. Roll one up and light it!" said Shawn.

Darius got up and walked toward the door.

"Where are you going, Darius?" Kenny asked.

"To the bathroom," he lied.

"Okay. Just hurry back. And don't wake my mother." Kenny's eyes fixated on the drugs. "The birthday boy goes first!" He reached for the bag.

Darius had seen enough. He wanted to go home, so he walked upstairs with every intention of never returning. First, he used his cell phone to call home. When he didn't get an answer, he went into the coat closet and grabbed his coat. Then, he surreptitiously opened the front door and walked out.

The temperature had begun to drop. Once outside, he walked swiftly, but he started shivering as the air got colder and colder.

The same white man who had made Linda uncomfortable spotted Darius out of his bedroom window. He picked up his firearm—which was conveniently placed on his dresser—and made sure it was loaded.

He grabbed a jacket on his way outside and sprinted after Darius. "Hey! What are you doing around here, boy?" he called out, still running behind him.

Darius started to walk even faster.

"What are you doing wandering around my neighborhood?" he called out again. He caught up to Darius and grabbed at his clothing to prevent him from running away. He got a handful of coat, but Darius managed to pull free. He chased Darius again and grabbed onto his shoulder with one hand, while tightening the grip on his pistol with the other hand. He spun Darius around.

A scuffle ensued. Darius struck out with a closed fist, causing the man to become dazed and temporarily see double. As a result, he aimed his pistol and fired a shot, but missed.

Scared for his life, Darius grabbed the man. In the mist of their grappling, the gun was fired a second time.

This time, the shot was a fatal one.

Neither man said a word. The narrow-minded man only smiled as he stared into Darius's frantic eyes. Then, the man collapsed on the cold concrete, as blood rushed from his chest wound.

Darius's heart was racing. He felt like it was going to beat out of his chest. He tried to remember CPR from a Law & Order episode he seen on television. He kneeled down to check the man's pulse, only to realize there wasn't any.

"Get away from him!" a man's voice shouted from behind him.

Another man from the neighborhood arrived on the scene. As he got closer, he pulled his gun and aimed it at Darius's head. He pulled the trigger, but no bullet was fired.

Darius had an angel watching over him.

There weren't any bullets in the gun. Unbeknownst to his father, earlier in the week, the man's teenage son had gone behind his back and done some target shooting with the pistol. He'd forgotten to reload it. The son's negligence saved Darius's life.

The man with the gun sized Darius up and decided that he had to come up with a ploy. Otherwise, he might lose his life, as well. "Freeze!" He pointed the empty gun at Darius.

"Please, don't shoot!"

"Stay right there, motherfucker." He reached in his pocket for a handkerchief, then kneeled down to pick up the murder weapon. He tucked his gun away and pointed the murder weapon at Darius. He then pulled out his cell phone and dialed 911.

He told the operator that Darius was black and that he'd killed a man. A patrol car arrived, and an officer was reading him his Miranda rights within minutes.

Shortly after Darius was detained, Linda was informed that Darius was in police custody. She listened to the officer describe the severity of the crime, but she could not believe her ears.

As Linda was getting dressed, all she could do was pray that everything would be all right.

Once she arrived at the precinct, she was told that Darius had been charged with homicide. voluntarily confessed to a murder and that he would have to wait to see a judge before being given bail. He would have to sit in jail until he was proven innocent. They knew that, to the judge and jury, he was already guilty.

CHAPTER 18

C orrectional officers in the Riverhead, New York, detention center had been harassing Darius. He had become their latest punching bag, since the last inmate they'd abused had been put into a coma and transferred, on life support, to an outside hospital. It hadn't even been a full two days, and Darius had already garnered an unfavorable reputation for himself. The officers had quickly acquired a dislike for him, upon realizing that he was the guy that had been involved in the death of their fellow correctional officer.

Today, Linda and Madeline were visiting. They endured being frisked for contraband before they were granted access into the visiting room to wait for Darius's arrival. The room had a plethora of people from different walks of life, all of them looking forward to seeing their loved ones.

An agitated African-American lady in her early twenties was sitting beside Linda. She was waiting on her boyfriend, whom she came to visit twice a week, to deliver contraband to him. Usually, she was relaxed, but today was different; she felt like she was being watched. She decided to get up and make her final exit. She was tired of the stagnant situation. Lately, she had been reading a self-help book that was supposed to empower women; she could honestly notice a difference in her confidence. All her boyfriend used to do was make her feel insecure with his verbal abuse. She didn't need his crap anymore. As she was within a few feet of the exit, though, she heard him call out to her.

"Sheryl!" he shouted, causing the overzealous correctional officer to lash out at him.

"No shouting in here, Jamal. You know that," he said. He pointed to a sign with red letters posted on the wall: No Shouting.

Actually, correctional officer Dunn usually used profanity, but he tailored his language during visiting hours. He wanted to appear professional, but outside of visiting hours, he was notorious for being both verbally and physically abusive toward the inmates.

"I'm sorry. It will not happen again," the prisoner said.

Officer Dunn just nodded his head. Normally, he would cancel an inmate's visit or cut it short if he violated the rules, but he received a tip from an informant that Jamal was going to be involved in a drug transaction. Sheryl walked back over to her seat. Although she did not want to admit it, he still had control over her.

"Where the hell did you think you were going?"

She felt compelled to look him in the eyes and tell him that she was finished with him.

It was a mistake that she would pay for.

She had finally decided that she was leaving him for good. Her family had stopped talking to her, because they thought her boyfriend was a bad influence over her.

Jamal noticed her air of confidence. He realized that his influence must be starting to dwindle; she hadn't been that confident since they'd first met. She clearly needed to be reprogrammed. He would start the process shortly.

"I was going home because I've had enough of this, Jamal. My own family doesn't talk to me because of this toxic relationship."

"Who the hell do you think you are talking to? You haven't had enough until I say you've had enough. Now apologize."

She looked around the visiting room to see if anyone was paying attention to the way he was speaking to her. Her eyes met the gaze of another lady who was there to see her husband. The lady shook her head. Sheryl didn't know it, but that lady was staring into a mirror and looking at her own reflection. Her husband had been going back and forth to prison for about twelve years. Now she had an idea of how foolish she looked from the outside looking in.

"I'm sorry," she said, as her newfound, empowered personality shed a tear.

"Stop with that crying shit! I done told you about that. Suck it up."

"I . . . I can't help it."

"Stop! You are drawing attention." Her newfound confidence had dwindled down to nothing. It made him smile. He loved being in control.

"I'm sorry," she said.

"I know you are. Just give me what you came to give me, and I will see you again in a few days."

She reached in her panties and pulled out a small balloon filled with marijuana. But this time, instead of putting the contraband in her mouth, then kissing him to transfer it from her mouth into his, her emotions got the best of her. She threw it in his face and stormed to the door.

"I'm sorry I fell in love with an insensitive jerk," she shouted.

Officer Dunn got what he was looking for. He escorted the inmate into solitary confinement. Due to the drama in the visiting room, Jamal would potentially be facing an additional sentence. Sheryl was apprehended as soon as she walked out of the room. She was given a green prison uniform and scheduled to see a judge in the morning. An example was made out of the couple; it deterred other couples from doing the same thing that evening.

About five minutes after the scene, Darius walked out, wearing a green prison uniform. Linda and Madeline could not help but notice the huge white bandage on the side of his head. Darius gave both Madeline and his Aunt a hug by reaching over the plexiglass partition, but Linda cut it short; she knew that too much contact was frowned upon by the correctional staff.

A slim correctional officer assigned to Darius kept a close watch on the trio. "What happened to your head?" Madeline asked, a mixture of anger and concern in her tone.

He looked around and saw the correctional officer shoot him a foreboding look. Darius did not want to be physically assaulted after his visit. He didn't know how many more beatings his body could withstand. He trembled as he looked away from the correctional officer and turned back to Madeline.

"I-I slipped and fell in the shower," he stammered.

"You slipped and fell," she repeated.

"Darius, don't fib. This is very serious," Linda said.

The officer gave Darius a subtle sneer. He seemed content with the boy's explanation.

But Madeline was not gullible. She detected abuse. She asked the question again. This time Darius started crying. It was a telltale sign of confirmation; he was being abused.

The correctional officer sprinted over to the table. He had to prevent Darius from saying anything that might cause an investigation. "This visit is over," he said abruptly. He reached under Darius's arms to force him to stand.

"But we just got here," Linda protested.

"That's too bad, ma'am. Darius, stand up!" With a tilt of his head, he signaled another officer for assistance. The other correctional officer was gung ho when it came to physical abuse of an inmate, so he rushed over.

"This isn't right!"

"Aunt Linda . . ."

"It's okay, Darius. You just listen to what the officers tell you." She glared at the slim correctional officer. "I would like to speak with your supervisor."

"You're speaking to him now." A stout man in a white shirt approached and winked at her.

"What happened to—"

Her question was cut off when the warden lifted his hand and signaled for a third officer. "Escort these women out!"

"Yes, sir. Women, right this way," the additional officer said as he led them out of the visiting room.

They knew Darius was being treated poorly. The only thing they could do now was speak to their lawyer, which they would do right away, or at least, once they were given their cell phones back. Cell phones were considered contraband, so they'd been taken when Madeline and Linda had arrived.

"Aunt Linda, don't leave me," Darius pleaded. He remained seated on the other side of the partition, despite the efforts of the two officers.

Other prisoners and visitors directed their attention toward the group. Once the warden noticed this, he grabbed Darius by the arm and yanked him upward to his feet.

The warden and the two correctional officers escorted Darius back to his cell. "We'll be back, Darius. Just listen to what they tell you to do," Linda said, as she and Madeline waved goodbye.

"I miss my mom." A tear rolled down his face.

His head was pounding. He still had a migraine from last night's beating, and he knew that the merciless warden and his minions who masqueraded as correctional officers would make life difficult for him tonight, just like they'd promised. As soon as the warden had Darius away from the visiting room—in handcuffs, of course—he slapped the boy across the face, causing tears to surface in his eyes. That was just the beginning of the assault. The worst was yet to come.

"I told you not to tell your loved ones what we've been doing to your retarded ass, but you didn't listen. I bet that, next time, you will learn to keep your big lips closed!" He rubbed his hands together and glared at Darius.

"Please, don't hurt me," Darius begged.

"Silence! Boys, you know what to do. I have to leave early tonight; I have a meeting with the brotherhood."

The warden was the imperial wizard of the Ku Klux Klan in Long Island, and he was already running late for his monthly meeting. Tonight, they would decide which black civil rights activist had to disappear next.

CHAPTER 19

February 27, 2015

Coram Plaza, Coram, New York

*L*eon pulled up in front of the Capital One Bank, accompanied by two acquaintances, Skip and Denise. Denise was Skip's pregnant, live-in girlfriend. Neither man seemed concerned with the fact that she was a-week-and-a-half shy of being nine months pregnant; their only concern was getting some quick cash. Skip was a seasonal landscaper who was currently unemployed, so he needed the heist to hold him over until he began working again.

Leon was suffering from withdrawal. He was so desperate that he'd decided spontaneously to pull off a heist at a local bank. He'd often thought about it before, but never imagined he would become desperate enough to actually do it.

Denise, thirty-four and unemployed, was a former employee at the bank. She'd been let go right after spurning her supervisor's sexual advances. He was a rich snob, accustomed to getting what he wanted—until he'd met Denise. He had a fascination with pregnant women, especially when they began to show. Since she did not want to have sex with him, as soon as she'd been tardy to work—the first time in five years—he'd fired her.

This morning, Denise was the getaway driver, and Leon and Skip were going to rob the bank. Both men were armed.

It was 9:30 AM, the bank opened at 10 AM. They sat in the parking lot and watched, as Denise named each employee who walked inside.

"There's Ellen. That's Cathy, and that's the bastard who fired me, Jonathan," she said, as she spoke through her teeth.

A half hour later, the bank was open to the public. The bank tellers were ready for another monotonous day of counting money. Little did they know that today would be a bit more exciting. Denise pulled up to the front entrance, then gave Skip a kiss for good luck. Leon rolled his eyes at their display of affection, but it made him think about his love. Heroin. From time to time, he thought about Valerie, but for all the wrong reasons. He thought about her when he was badly in need of a fix, because, if she were still alive, she could turn tricks for some quick cash to support their habit. Lately, he had been doing a lot of robberies.

Averting his eyes, he looked out the window.

He didn't want to get too emotional, so he focused on the task at hand.

"Skip, let's go." His tone reflected the fact that his patience was wearing thin.

"I'm coming, man."

Both men covered their faces with black ski masks, grabbed their empty bags, and concealed their guns. It was show time.

From the very moment that the two men entered the bank, they did everything precisely as planned. Leon locked the top lock on the door, then each man reached for his weapon and ran up to the bank tellers with demands.

"Listen up!" Leon said. "If anyone signals the cops, I promise that people will die this morning. Everyone, kiss the floor, except for the two bank tellers."

The manager and the two other bank employees did as they were told.

"All we ask for is your cooperation, and everyone will be all right and able to go home to their families," Skip said.

Leon's teller was a blond, thirty-seven-year-old mother of two. She and her husband had just had a newborn; they had a lot to live for, so she was willing to comply.

But the bank manager was not. In fact, he had already signaled for the police, right after having heard Leon shout listen up.

"I will do whatever you want me to do," the teller said, trying her best to remain calm.

"I like you already." He handed her his bag.

In less than three minutes, the men were in and out, as planned.

As soon as they stepped outside, however, they were greeted with a heavy police presence. Their getaway driver was sitting in the back of an ambulance, one hand cuffed to the stretcher. She had gone into an early labor. Unfortunately, she would not be present to witness her baby girl take her first steps.

"Drop your weapons!" an officer shouted at them.

There was nowhere to run; they were besieged with blue uniforms. Realizing that there was no escape route, both men surrendered without further incident. After dropping their weapons, they were handcuffed and placed under arrest.

CHAPTER 20

$\mathcal{T}$oday, Linda and Madeline were visiting Darius with their court-appointed attorney, Mr. Farley. Their attorney looked like he had been deprived of sleep. His clothes were in need of an iron, and he had traces of white powder on the edge of his nostrils, which gave credence to the rumor that he got high. Linda and Madeline wished that they had better legal representation, but for now, he was their only hope. Although he seemed indifferent to Darius's plight, they didn't have much of a choice, since their resources were limited.

They wanted answers. They knew that Darius was being abused by the staff, and they wanted to make sure that it came to a halt. Upon arrival, they took notice of the staff's, awkward silence now that an attorney was present. They were met by the warden.

Farley rubbed his nose, then stepped forward until he was face to face with the warden. "We are here to see Darius Robinson," he stated, trying to be aggressive, but falling short.

"Mr. Robinson told us that he does not want to see anyone today," the warden lied.

Linda took issue with this. "I find that very difficult to believe. My nephew is always excited to see his family."

"I can't force him to come down here if he refuses," the warden explained.

They reached a standstill. Linda and Madeline looked to Mr. Farley "Mr. Farley! You're bleeding," Madeline said.

He reached for his hanky and applied it to his nostril. "I'm sorry.

This has been happening a lot, lately. I need to go to the restroom," he told them.

They felt like they weren't going to get very far, so they decided to leave peacefully under the aegis of Mr. Farley.

The whole situation was outrageous. Why would Darius refuse to see them? But there was nothing they could do, except wait for him to phone home, which he hadn't been doing lately, or wait for his next court appearance, which was in two weeks.

Unfortunately, he would not have the chance to appear before the judge. The day before his next court appearance, Linda got a call from Mr. Farley, informing her that Darius had committed suicide. He'd been found in his cell, dead from asphyxiation. He'd hung himself with his bed sheets.

He had left a note behind. With access to a Webster's dictionary and help from an inmate in a neighboring cell, he'd written his final letter.

Of course, his aunt would never receive that letter; the correctional officers made sure of it. They ripped it up and flushed it down the toilet.

March 12, 2015

Dear Aunt Linda,

People in here are being mean to me. I can't take it anymore. Did you find my puppy? How come you and Madeline don't visit or write me anymore? Don't you guys love me? Have you heard from my dad? I'm lonely, and I miss Uncle Robert. The warden and the correctional officers told me that my family and friends forgot about me. I hope that isn't true. I can hardly sleep at night, because the correctional officers keep coming into my cell and throwing buckets of cold water on me in the middle of the night. Please, get me out of here before I kill myself, Aunt Linda.

Love,

Darius

PROLOGUE

March 12, 2016

One year and a slew of lawsuits later, Linda and other African-American families who'd lost loved ones to police brutality were several million dollars richer—but the money still did not make up for their losses.

Recently, the media had covered a large scandal that involved corrupt officers, judges, and politicians. The jig was up: a large media presence stood right outside of Chief Murphy's home. After several decades, his corrupt lifestyle had finally caught up with him. He would be held accountable for a list of illegal actions, including witness tampering and drug trafficking. The thought of prison life caused him to go out of his mind. The inmates will kill me, he thought. He and his peers were the reason that thousands of inmates had been wrongfully convicted and given a disproportionate jail sentence.

When the police arrived to apprehend Chief Murphy at his home in Dix Hills, Long Island, they found him dead in his bedroom. Apparently, he'd locked himself in his bedroom, put the barrel of a gun in his mouth, and committed suicide, just when the officers had been knocking on his door. By his side, they found a brief suicide note: *I would rather kill myself before being brought to justice and giving satisfaction to the thousands of black American citizens I'd robbed of their loved ones. White power!*

The contents of the note was immediately leaked to a news reporter standing outside Chief Murphy's home.

The congressman and the district attorney were being arraigned in court and prosecuted, along with many of their peers. The various sections of New York State that they'd once ruled would be improving.

Leon was incarcerated. He would be serving eight years for the bank robbery. Robert's former security team were all convicted on conspiracy charges in connection with aiding and abetting his death. They were given a total of three hundred years behind bars. Jacob, the head of security and Robert's friend since kindergarten, would never step outside of prison again. After two months of incarceration, he was found stabbed to death in his cell. His killer was never found.

In the interim, Linda decided to sell the house and downsize to a one-bedroom apartment.

Today, she was moving her belongings in. She was beginning to love life again, and the urge to cause herself bodily harm was gone. Seven months ago, she'd attempted to take her life again, using the pistol, but she'd sensed her husband's spirit in the bedroom. It had seemed as if he'd actually been there. She'd felt his spirit remove the gun from her head and guide her to place it back in the safe, where it belonged. That was confirmation to her that he was watching over her.

The U-Haul sat parked outside the Carter residence. Linda picked up the last box, filled with family photos and other memorabilia, and carried it outside to the truck.

"Is that the last box?" Madeline asked on her way into the house.

"Yes."

Linda then placed it on the back of the truck and pulled down the latch to close it.

"So, this is it, huh?" Madeline said.

Linda glanced around the yard.

"Yes. I think it's for the best. It's really hard for me to continue to live here; everything is a trigger for me. It makes me depressed."

"I understand."

The women then made their way back into the house.

Robert's coffee mug—#1 Uncle—was on the window sill; steam was rising from it, as if someone were using it. Linda's jaw dropped as she stared at the mug, then blinked in disbelief. She looked as if she had seen a ghost. Chills ran up her spine.

"Madeline, how did this get here?" she gestured to the cup. "I know that I packed it in a box with all his other things."

"That's weird. I didn't put it there." She shrugged her shoulders. "Then who did?"

Both women teared up, then embraced. They didn't need to answer that question; they could feel Robert's presence in the room.

Suddenly, the front door closed. The women flinched.

Robert and Darius began to walk down the street, as they took Buddy for his walk. The afterlife was treating them both well. They'd already been promoted and gotten their wings, due to all of the good deeds that they'd done in heaven during the year. It took most spirits several years to become an angel, so this was a huge accomplishment.

"Uncle, why can't Madeline and Aunt Linda see us? I tried giving her a hug earlier, and she didn't hug me back."

"Because you, Buddy, and I are spirits now. We are here to try our best to watch over Madeline and Aunt Linda and to make sure that the bad people don't harm her, like they harmed us. When it's their time to go, there is nothing that we can do about it, but until then, we will be their guardian angels."

"Cool, Uncle Robert! On TV, guardian angels have halos on top of their heads; how come we don't have ours?"

Robert smiled. "Darius, on television, things are make-believe. For example, on television, God is represented as being Caucasian, but when God gave us our wings, we both saw that he was the same complexion as we are and that his hair was the same texture as ours. Son, you can't believe everything that you hear on television." He placed his hands on the boy's shoulders.

"Okay, Uncle Robert."

Robert looked at his watch and realized he was running late.

"So, Darius, I have to get ready to meet up with some friends for dinner."

"Okay. I have to meet two of my friends at the basketball court. Trayvon Martin invited me to play a game of horse with him and Mike Brown."

Oh, when you're smiling,
When you're smiling,
The whole world smiles with you. . . .

Robert walked into the upscale restaurant and heard one of his favorite songs playing. He was surprised when he looked over and saw who was singing. The piano and trumpet blended so beautifully together. Then he walked toward a cordial host.

Yes, when you're laughing, when you're laughing,
Yes, the sun comes shining through. . . .

"Good evening. You must be Robert Carter," he said.

"Good evening." He frowned. "How do you know who I am?"

"I've heard a lot about you, sir. It's a pleasure."

The men shook hands.

"I have a question: Is that Louis Armstrong singing?"

The host smiled and nodded his head. "Come right this way; your table is ready."

But when you're crying,
You bring on the rain.
So stop your sighing, baby,
And be happy again. . . .

As Robert was making his way to his table, bobbing his head to the jazz music, he heard a man boasting about being the greatest of all time. The voice sounded familiar. When he looked at the man who was speaking, his mouth dropped open. Rocky Marciano and Muhammad

Ali were having dinner! He waved, and the two men waved back and smiled.

Yes, and keep on smiling,
Keep on smiling,
And the whole world smiles with you!

"This is your table, Mr. Carter," the gentleman said.

At the table, three men were already seated, awaiting Robert's arrival. A militant black gentleman, dressed predominantly in black from head to toe, stood up to greet Robert with a long-anticipated, firm handshake. On his beret was a symbol of a large cat, which communicated his affiliation with the civil rights group, the Black Panthers, which advocated Black Nationalism.

"Robert Carter, it is a pleasure to finally get the chance to meet you! My name is Fred Hampton, and these two gentlemen are Dr. Martin Luther King Jr and Malcolm X."

ABOUT THE AUTHOR

Lloyd Williams is an American author from Long Island, NY. Because he grew up under-privileged, his past was no walk in the park. As the second oldest of seven children, he was raised in a single-parent household. His mother struggled to take care of him and his siblings, as his father came and went. Frequently moving from despair-ridden place to place gave him inspiration and the insight he needed to articulate his stories. In 2015, at the age of 29, he self-published his first book, *Stephanie's Diary*, and he has already gathered a dedicated fan base.

Contact Info: Authorlloydwilliams@gmail.com
Facebook/Instagram @Authorlloydwilliams